THE Hebrew Kid
and the Apache Maiden

By
Robert J. Avrech

SERAPHIC PRESS

SERAPHIC PRESS
1531 Cardiff Avenue
Los Angeles, California 90035

Jacket & page design by Lanphear Design
Jacket illustrations & chapter illustrations by
Obadinah Heavner, copyright © 2005 Obadinah Heavner
Calligraphy by Iskra
Type is set in Janson Text
Chapter titles are set in Caslon Antique

ISBN 0-9754382-1-2
Printed in the USA
Library of Congress Control Number: 2004107456
First Edition

LIBRARY OF CONGRESS CATALOGING-IN-PUBLICATION DATA

Avrech, Robert J. (Robert Joel), 1950-
The Hebrew Kid and the Apache Maiden /
by Robert J. Avrech.- 1st ed.
p. cm.
ISBN 0-9754382-1-2 (alk. paper)
1. Lozen–Fiction. 2. Apache women–Fiction.
3. Women soldiers–Fiction.
4. Jews–Arizona–Fiction. 5. Boys–Fiction. I. Title.
PS3601.V74H43   2005
813'.6–dc22
2004015237

In Memory of
Ariel Chaim Avrech

My Son
My Teacher
My Inspiration

❦

Table of Contents

THE Hebrew Kid and the Apache Maiden

Chapter 1
—· Into the Whirlwind ·—

The night the town threatened to burn us out, I was preparing for my bar mitzvah. More than anything, I wanted to be a man, to take my place in the community of Jews. Unfortunately, Papa had brought us to a place where there were no Jews.

Papa was saying Ma'ariv, the evening prayer, when they came knocking at the door. Rebecca looked up from the cooking pit where she was preparing dinner. Oblivious, Papa swayed to and fro. He did not hear the insistent knocks, the warped door rattling on its leather hinges. Papa was reaching out to heaven, and nothing could penetrate his spiritual shelter.

I opened the door.

The mayor of our town, Thomas Wilberforce, filled the narrow doorway. Mrs. Blake and Mrs. Slocum were right behind him; their sharp chins thrust out over the starched black collars of their coats.

"Is your Pa to home?" Mayor Wilberforce asked.

"He is davening—I mean, praying."

Wilberforce heaved a frustrated sigh. He claimed that he respected our faith, but whenever he was confronted with the concrete reality of our traditions, I could see the tense discomfort in his eyes.

"We'll wait."

"Would you like to come in?"

"We're fine just where we are."

In all the time we had lived in this small Arizona town, the mayor had never entered our home. Rebecca said that he was afraid of being tainted by the very air we breathed. Nobody could believe such foolishness, I said. Rebecca leveled a severe gaze at me and lifted a single eyebrow, silently telling me that I was a naïve and ignorant child. In my heart, I knew that she was right, but admitting such a thing was simply too awful; it was too painful to think that such things could be believed here in America, our new home, the Golden Land. I expected, even accepted as natural, such hateful attitudes back in Europe, but here in this, our marvelous new country? No, no, I did not want to acknowledge it.

Gazing at the grim figures, dark shadows barely shifting in the doorway, I could sense that they brought bad tidings. Papa had gone against the wishes of the town, and they were not going to stand for it. Least of all from us. Strangers. Foreigners. Jews.

Their breaths created small white clouds that formed, collided and disintegrated. Wilberforce and the good ladies looked like dark angels breathing white fire.

Papa took three small steps back and then three steps forward. He bowed to the east and then to the west. He was finished with the Shmoneh Esrei, the Eighteen Benedictions. I spoke in Yiddish.

"They're here, Papa."

He closed his eyes and dipped his head—just once—to let me know that he was well aware of their presence. He stroked his beard and said the Alenu, the final prayer of the evening service.

Rebecca stirred the cast iron cooking pot. She spoke in English. Some people said that Rebecca's Russian accent could barely be detected. She had a talent for languages.

"You should know by now, you can't hurry him. This shack could be falling down and he wouldn't even notice. And speak English; we are in America now."

Rebecca was angry with Papa. It seemed that she was always annoyed with him. "He needs," she said, "to get his head out of the clouds and his feet back to earth."

Papa smoothed his black caftan. It shone like sealskin under the rays of silvery moonlight that slipped through the cracks in the sod roof. He went to the door, straightened his shoulders. "Mayor Wilberforce, good evening to you."

Wilberforce's tone was cold as the air. "Mr. Isaacson."

It made me so angry. Papa was given semicha, rabbinic ordination, from the great and pious Rabbi Velvel Soloveitchik. Why couldn't they pay him the courtesy of calling him Rabbi? Whenever I complained about this, Papa just smiled and ran his hand over my cheek. "What does it matter?" he would say.

"Ah, Mrs. Blake, Mrs. Slocum, won't you come in? Please, please, it is so very cold outside. Rebecca, my child, prepare some tea for our guests." Papa was unfailingly polite.

Mrs. Slocum's lips contracted into two white lines.

"This is not a social visit."

"No, it most certainly is not," chimed Mrs. Blake. The women were rigid and self-righteous.

Larke Ellen's baby started to cry. I could hear Mama, in the bedroom, cooing to the newborn in Yiddish.

Mayor Wilberforce stiffened, hooked his thumbs into his vest pockets. Behind him the moon was thick and swollen, like a silver dollar nailed into the black sky.

"Now, Mr. Isaacson, we warned you about opening a business here."

"But Mayor," Papa said, "How can I make a living if I do not ply my trade?"

"We already got a boot maker," said Wilberforce.

"Murphy sells dry goods and some shoes," said Papa. "I am a custom boot maker."

"Nevertheless…" said Wilberforce.

"Surely there is room for both of us. In fact, we complement each other. Murphy sends business my way, and I do the same for him."

Wilberforce looked past Papa to the back room where Larke Ellen was resting on the rope bed.

"Is she in a bad way?"

"Recovering. Slowly recovering."

"That's another thing. No one holds with a Christian girl working for people like you."

"Larke Ellen is a poor widow. She begged us for work. How else will she be able to eat, to feed her baby?" replied Papa.

Wilberforce said sternly, "The good citizens of this town are determined to set a good example for our children."

"Is not kindness a good thing to show children?"

Wilberforce spit, releasing a squirt of tobacco juice into the hard-packed dirt floor, just beyond Papa's foot. Papa pretended not to notice.

"We're not here to argue, Isaacson. We know what's right and what ain't. We are trying to establish a decent society here. It's hard enough contending with the Apaches, them redskin savages; we surely do not need your kind stirring things up. We want you and your family to be out of this community by sunrise, y'hear?"

Rebecca gasped. Papa frowned, as if he didn't quite understand what he was being told. I felt my heart beating in my chest like a trapped bird.

"But Larke Ellen is terribly weak," protested Rebecca. "It was a difficult birth. There was a great deal of blood, a great deal. You must know that she almost died."

"We will watch over her," said Mrs. Blake.

"Perhaps you should speak to Larke Ellen about this. Naturally, whatever she decides will be fine by us," Papa said.

"If Larke Ellen got a lick of sense she'll choose her own," said Mrs. Slocum.

There was a long moment of silence.

"And if we do not go?" Papa finally said.

Wilberforce lit a cigar. He blew out a blue cloud of smoke, then stared at the burning match. The tense angle of his jaw looked sculpted from a wedge of marble.

"Got to be careful of fire," said Wilberforce.

Wilberforce leveled his glance at Papa and continued very quietly, "One match can wipe out a lifetime of work." The lit match fell from his fingers, flared brightly for a second before I stepped forward and stamped out the flame.

Papa didn't answer the implied threat.

Without another word, Wilberforce and the women turned and marched away. They melted into dark, floating objects against the dusky northern sky. Papa shut the cabin door. It groaned on its hinges, battered by a gust of stiff wind. Sharp branches of cottonwood scraped against the outside walls, and somewhere in the distance a prairie dog howled. It sounded almost human, like a crying woman.

"Papa?" Mama's voice was tense and helpless. She was standing in the bedroom doorway. Larke Ellen's baby was cradled in her arms, sleeping peacefully. A tiny fist rose and fell. Papa turned around and faced Mama. Their eyes met. He shook his head helplessly.

"No," cried Rebecca. "It's not fair."

"No, it is not fair," agreed Papa.

"We should go to the sheriff," said Mama.

Rebecca snorted. "The sheriff is a useless fool. He does what Wilberforce and the others tell him to do. The only thing he's good for is shooting stray dogs."

"And he's not even good at that," I said. "He's usually too drunk to shoot straight."

"What are we going to do, Papa?" Mama cried.

Larke Ellen's baby wailed, startled by Mama's outburst. To soothe the infant, Mama touched the baby's little mouth with her forefinger, lips as smooth and shiny as boiled candy. As if by enchantment, the baby gurgled like a pigeon.

"I think we should pack," said Papa.

◎　◎　◎

Rebecca was flinging her clothing into the horsehair trunk. She brushed away the tears that streaked her face.

"It's all his fault," she said.

"Who?"

"Papa, who else? Opening the business, hiring Larke Ellen. I told him not to. I told him it was a mistake."

"You're not being fair. Papa was doing a mitzvah hiring Larke Ellen, and how else can he make a living but making boots?"

"He's always doing mitzvahs, and we always end up suffering for it."

"You shouldn't say things like that."

"Why not?"

"Because it's not true."

"I knew this was going to happen," she said. "I just knew it."

I only had two shirts: a threadbare, butternut-colored

boiled wool shirt, which I was wearing, and a white one for Shabbos. I rolled my good shirt and shoved it into a corner of the trunk. Rebecca frowned.

"Can't you fold? What's wrong with you men? We've moved enough that you should know how to do it by now." She pulled out my Shabbos shirt and gingerly folded it. "There, you little troublemaker," she said. "Now it won't get so creased."

She turned and gazed into her looking glass. The mirror was aged, fractured like marble with spider webs of silver and gray. She scowled. "Look at my hair, I just did it and now it will get ruined." Rebecca wore her hair divided in three sections, with a pewter comb at the back and, at the sides, a tangle of dense curls. She had patiently turned the ringlets with a hot iron, having first made her hair wet with a mixture of sugar and water. The curls would stiffen like the bark of a tree and the effect would last for about a week. Mama thought the style too fancy, meaning not modest enough, but Rebecca firmly insisted that it was the American style. It was the fashion, and my seventeen-year-old sister was determined to be a real American girl. Mama spit three times and murmured, "God forbid, God forbid."

Rebecca put a hand to her hair and patted it into place. She had long delicate fingers ridged with pale blue veins. Her hands were soft and white in spite of all the sewing and cooking she did. So pale were her hands, they seemed to shine, smooth as ivory or alabaster. Every evening, to keep her skin smooth, Rebecca coated her hands with chicken fat and then wore gloves all night long. My sister was proud of her hands; she vowed that someday she would go to an ice cream social, and all the young men would admire her beautiful skin.

After helping Papa pack the books—he handled each volume as if it were a bar of gold—I went to see if Mama needed my help with anything. She was wrapping the baby in a flannel blanket. Larke Ellen sat on the edge of the bed. Thread thin and freckled, she was flushed with fever. Her red hair lay in damp tangles over her shoulders. It was only twelve hours ago that she lay shrieking on the thin straw mattress. Her labor had been prolonged and painful. The baby was facing the wrong direction, but Mama had managed to turn it around. Finally, the baby was born in a huge surge of blood.

"Larke Ellen," said Papa, "they have told us we have to leave."

"I heard," she replied.

"But you will be taken care of. They promised to take care of you and the baby."

Larke Ellen shook her head from side to side.

"No, I ain't stayin' here. Please, let me come with you. You folks took me in and gave me work and showed kindness when no one else would."

"But we must travel, and you are so weak."

"You treat me good and fair; I may be poor Kansas trash to the rest of the good folks in this town, but you always treated me like a lady. I got faults, Lord knows, but disloyalty ain't one of them. I'm coming with you and ain't nothing gonna stop me."

"But Larke Ellen," interjected Mama, "surely you want to stay with your own people, don't you?"

"They ain't my people. Never have been. You're my people now—if you'll continue to have me."

Papa and Mama exchanged questioning looks. Mama sighed and Papa shrugged his shoulders. Larke Ellen was right; she was one of us, in her own way.

Larke Ellen leaned over to button her shoes, but the effort was too much for her aching body. She winced, stopped by a solid wall of pain, sluggishly straightened up and gripped the edges of the bunk in order to regain her balance.

"I can't seem to manage," she murmured.

"Ariel, give Larke Ellen a hand." Mama ordered.

I kneeled and buttoned Larke Ellen's black boots. The leather was cracked, like parched desert clay, and at least two sizes too big. Papa was working on new boots for her.

"I'm sorry," said Larke Ellen, to no one in particular.

"Sha," Mama counseled, "sha-shtill, save your strength."

"Awful sorry," Larke Ellen repeated. Her voice was low and hopeless. "When Billy died the whole world seemed to go bad for me. Lord forgive me, but I even gave thought to taking my own life. But the good book says that taking your own life will send you on a freight train straight to hell. The preacher back home once said that even thinking of it is a mortal sin. You reckon he's right, Mrs. Isaacson? You reckon I'm going to burn in hell with all them evil sinners? Is that to be my fate, my final judgment?"

Mama heaved a sigh as she threw a woolen shawl over Larke Ellen's narrow shoulders. In Yiddish Mama said, "Who knows what God does with goyim?"

◎ ◎ ◎

I carried a shuttered lantern outside and hitched the team to the wagon.

Memories came flooding back. The last pogrom drove us out of our village, out of Russia, out of Europe. It was during Yom Kippur that the Cossacks rode into our shtetl. They thundered in, mounted on screaming horses, hundreds of barbarous warriors. Their curved swords hacked and stabbed. Their guns let loose countless deadly volleys. "Hep, hep, hep," they cried. Men, women and children were slaughtered like animals. Our beautiful wooden synagogue, over seven hundred years old, burned like a torch. Orange flames and pillars of black smoke climbed to the sky. The Cossacks trampled on the holy Torah scrolls. The ground was soaked in innocent blood, and the mean stench of death filled our nostrils.

Somehow, we managed to escape into the woods. The Cossacks were too busy looting, raping and murdering to go after us. We survived in the forest for ten endless days and nights. We ate flowers, grass and tree bark. At night we slept in ditches, covered ourselves in leaves and shivered on the frozen earth. We dared not light a fire. Surely Cossack patrols were still in the area. We prayed. We mourned the death of our friends, our many relatives, and our poor village. On the tenth day in the forest, Papa told us of his dream. He saw us traveling across a great ocean. To where? To the golden land of America. Mama was horrified. "America," she wept, "we cannot go to America. It's a treif land," she insisted. Rebecca said nothing. She was in a state of shock. Mendel, the boy she was going to marry, had been murdered along with his entire family.

Papa told us that there were no Cossacks in America. He told us that we would be safe in America. But Mama continued to beg and plead. "Mama," Papa said in his most gentle voice, "we are going to America. We are going to be free. America is a wondrous land."

"But it's only a dream," Mama cried. "Who listens to dreams?"

"I do," said Papa.

Secretly, I was thrilled.

After a long and arduous journey over countless lands and seas, in the Christian year of 1870, we landed on the shores of America.

◎ ◎ ◎

The scrape of shoes against the hard earth brought me back to the Arizona Territory. I turned around to find myself face to face with Tucker, the mayor's fourteen-year-old son. He said, "Pa's runnin' you off, ain't he?"

I nodded.

"I'm real sorry. Ma's real unhappy too. Thinks it ain't Christian."

He stepped forward into a bar of moonlight. I could see that his left eye was swollen shut.

"Did your father do that?" I asked.

Tucker didn't answer. Instead, he handed me a carefully folded oilcloth. "Ma made some jerky and cornbread for Larke Ellen; will you give it to her?" I nodded and took the oilcloth. "Ma made plenty. Enough for you and your kin."

"We can't, Tucker. It's not kosher. I'm sorry."

Embarrassed, Tucker shook his head. "That's right. I plum forgot. Can't quite get the hang of them laws you got for food."

I smiled. No matter how many times I explained kashrus to Tucker, he was never quite able to comprehend its intricacies.

"Well, maybe your Pa can bless it and make it okay."

"That's not how it works, but thank you just the same."

Tucker frowned. He hesitated. Finally he came out with it. "Ma wants to know if Larke Ellen's staying in the settlement."

"No," I told him, "she wants to come with us. We told her to stay, but she doesn't want to."

"Did Larke Ellen name the baby yet?"

I shook my head.

"Nobody in town treated Larke Ellen and her husband good. They was just white trash farmers, and that husband of hers fought for the Union. This settlement is solid Confederate."

Papa and Mama also supported the Union, but we never said it out loud, not in a town where so many of the men were veterans of Robert E. Lee's vanquished army.

"Well, you take care; I hear tell that Victorio is awful riled up," said Tucker.

I shuddered. The very name of the fearsome Apache chief sent chills up my spine.

Tucker reached under his patched brown corduroy jacket and came up with a pistol. He offered it to me, butt first. I searched his eyes, questioning.

"Tucker?"

"Go on, take it."

"I cannot."

"You got to. How you going to make it through the territory without iron?"

"But Tucker, it is your gun."

"Aw hell, Ariel, you're gonna need it more than me. You can be darn sure of that. Look here, you're gonna protect Larke Ellen and your kin, ain't you?"

"I'm too young, Tucker."

"Too young? Hell, Ariel, ain't you heard? There ain't no boys west of the Mississippi."

I took the gun. Surprised by its considerable weight, I almost let it fall from my hands. Tucker grinned and slipped a handful of cartridges into my pocket. "That there's a Walker .44 caliber. Kicks like a mule. Remember to keep the chamber under the hammer empty so you don't go blowing your foot off. Shoots a might wide, about four feet, but she's a good old cannon. You treat her good and she'll do right by you." A thought suddenly occurred to Tucker. "Tell me something, you Jewish folks, you got any laws against killing?"

"We are not allowed to murder," I said.

Tucker stared at me, puzzled. "Kill, murder, don't see the difference."

"We are allowed to kill," I explained, "but only when our lives are threatened. To kill without a reason is murder. That's the Sixth Commandment: You shall not murder."

Tucker seemed relieved. "That's real sensible. But don't you go waiting too long before deciding that you're being mortal threatened," he cautioned. I smiled and shook my head in agreement. Tucker had a good point. It was something the rabbis of the Talmud had discussed in detail over a thousand years ago.

"And Ariel, don't you be calling it a gun. This here's a pistol. Only sorry tenderfoots call them guns."

"But Tucker, I am a tenderfoot."

"Shoot, that ain't for no one else to know. Far as everyone else is concerned you're, let me see..." Tucker frowned, his mind racing. And then he chuckled. "The Hebrew Kid, that's who you are: The Hebrew Kid, terror of the Arizona Territory."

"Oy vey," I said.

We both laughed. But the truth was I had never fired a gun in my life. Tucker had offered to let me fire it, pointing out that I was twelve years old and more than ready to learn the art of gun shooting. However, I had always declined. Bullets were too expensive.

I slipped the Walker into my waistband. Its solid heft almost pulled my pants down. I knew how much the revolver meant to Tucker. It had belonged to an Indian-fighting uncle of his who was murdered by the Apache.

Nervously, Tucker glanced over his shoulder. He was terrified that he would be discovered talking to me. His tone turned somber.

He extended his hand, and I took it.

"Where you figure to be heading?"

"I'm not sure, but I hope it's a place where I can have my bar mitzvah."

✽

Chapter 2

—· Kabbalah ·—

Wistfully Mama said, "This is what I get for marrying a mystic." She rolled up the kesubah, their marriage contract, slipped it inside its leather case and then packed it in the carpetbag. She took one last look around the sod shack we had called home for just ten months.

Outside, the church bell rang.

"Where are we going?" Mama asked Papa.

"I'll know when we get there."

Mama heaved a great sigh. That was not what she wanted Papa to say. Mama wanted a plan, something definite.

As we rode out of the settlement, a thin slice of light pressed up against the pale mountains. It was bitterly cold.

The wagon bounced along the rutted road, which ran down the center of the town. Some of our neighbors peeked out their windows; others stood in their doorways and watched us go. One of the town children threw a mud pie at us.

Papa's eyes were fixed on the far horizon. He was already

somewhere else. Mama looked angrily at the people of the settlement as they lined up to see us go.

"Shame on you," she cried. "For shame!"

Rebecca raised her shawl over her head to hide her tears. All she wanted, she said, was to have a home like everybody else, to stay in one place. Rebecca was tired of moving from settlement to settlement.

"Papa won't be happy until we end up in China," she said.

Papa's eyes lit up. "China, I wonder if there are any Jews in China," he mused. Rebecca cried out in frustration. "You see," she said, "you see!"

The rim of the bulging sun was spreading gold above the distant hills.

Passing the Wilberforce house, I saw the front door open and a frightened face peering out. It was Tucker's mother. After a brief moment, the door was violently slammed shut. I could hear Mayor Wilberforce's voice rising in anger.

Soon we were in the desert.

◙   ◙   ◙

The day and the miles wore on. The heat increased as the sun neared its zenith. I wiped my forehead with the sleeve of my shirt, but my skin was bone dry. It was so hot that the air sucked the moisture right out of my body.

The wagon wheels churned up great clouds of swirling dust that flogged the air and made it difficult to breathe. I wrapped a bandanna over my nose.

Papa was sitting on the wagon seat, an open book on his lap. He was absorbed in the Zohar, a grand and holy book of mystical thought: Kabbalah, something only the most brilliant men were encouraged to study, and then only if they were married with children. Larke Ellen sat in the back of the buckboard and held her baby. Mama, right beside Papa, drove the team of mules. Rebecca and I walked some twenty yards ahead of the wagon, clearing the path of large rocks and filling in ruts with shovels so the wagon wheels wouldn't get damaged. We were also on the lookout for rattlesnakes to make sure that the mules would not get bitten or spooked. Rebecca warned me that if we did see a rattlesnake, she planned to run away as fast as her legs would carry her. As we walked ahead of the wagon, Rebecca recited the names of the different places we had lived.

"Hoboken. Pittsburgh. Cincinnati. Wichita. Santa Fe..."

"You forgot Silver City."

"That's because we were only there for two hours."

"Papa said it was too dangerous with all the drunken miners."

"And traveling all alone through Indian territory, this isn't dangerous?"

I wasn't about to continue the argument, a familiar disagreement. Rebecca just didn't realize that Papa was special. Papa was different. He was on a mission to discover the Lamed Vovniks, the thirty-six righteous men who live in each generation on whose merits the world depends. One of these Lamed Vovniks is destined to be the Messiah—if the generation is worthy. According to Jewish tradition they wander in exile and only come forward when there is danger to a Jew or his community. It is said that they are all very poor. Also, they are forbidden from ever revealing themselves to others.

After the pogrom ripped our lives apart, Papa, who was always deeply immersed in mysticism, gradually became obsessed with the Lamed Vovniks. It was to me, one Shabbos evening, during our walk after dinner that Papa confided his plan to seek out the thirty-six, or at least just one of them.

"Hopefully," he whispered, "I will hasten the coming of the Messiah."

I remember looking up at Papa and feeling my heart swell with pride. To me he seemed as wise as King Solomon, as brave and heroic as King David.

◎ ◎ ◎

The blistering heat made it difficult to concentrate, and sometimes I would find myself walking along as if in a dream. And then there were the mirages. Visions. The heat waves shimmered. And every so often the quivering waves turned into lakes filled with clear, ice-cold water.

"Look," I would call out, "it's water." I'd run towards the glittering lake, and then it would disappear. The water turned to sand.

Shortly before noon we made a brief stop near a grove of saguaro cactus. The desert giants stood, some more than twenty feet high, with their limbs reaching skyward; they reminded me of men caught in prayer.

Mama sewed, repairing Papa's socks. Rebecca crawled under the wagon and lay there reading one of her storybooks. They were silly romances about knights and princesses. There was lots of kissing. I teased her every chance I got. But Rebecca would just turn up her nose and call me an ignorant child. I told Rebecca to read the stories of Mr. Charles Dickens, but Rebecca complained that his stories were too sad. Personally, I love Mr. Charles Dickens, and when I'm not learning Torah, I read his wonderful tales. It is also a fine way to learn the English language.

Papa opened a bottle of ink and continued work on his book, a mystical commentary on the book of Job. He had been writing his book for as long as I could remember. Mama said he would never finish it.

I unharnessed the weary team of mules. Papa was strict about the care of animals. "The Torah says that before you feed yourself, you must take care of the animals that work for you," he said. I fed the mules grain and water. Most people don't realize how smart mules are. A hungry horse will eat and drink until it gets sick. But a mule will take its time and eat just what it needs. A horse will run and run until it drops and dies. But a mule will stop when it's tired and go no further, no matter what you do to it.

Larke Ellen fed her baby in the shade of one of the saguaros. After she finished the feeding, I brought her a water bag.

"Mama says to drink."

Obediently, Larke Ellen tipped back her head and thirstily gulped down the water. I shared a small loaf of Mama's bread with Larke Ellen.

"I heard you talking to your pa about your bar... bar something."

"Bar mitzvah. It's a tradition that when a boy turns thirteen, he reads from the Torah, makes a little speech and is then considered a man."

"Do you reckon your folk'll let me stay with you, wherever you go?"

I shrugged. I had no idea what was planned. We wouldn't know until Papa had one of his dreams.

"After Billy passed on, I didn't know what I was going to do. The settlement never liked us because Billy rode with the Blue. Truth is, Billy didn't have no fixed notions on slavery. He just did what his pa told him. I figure it was that way for most of the poor boys what perished in the conflict."

"Billy was a fine man."

"He was better than most, not as good as some others. It was a hard death. Getting snake bit and poisoned."

Her eyes widened in alarm.

"Larke Ellen, what's wrong?"

"Look yonder—riders."

A funnel of yellow dust flowed towards us, and out of the cloud riders could be seen. They were riding hard. I called to Papa and he corked his jar of ink, carefully laid his papers aside, put on his frock coat, and brushed the silvery dust from the black wool. The mica particles lay on the ground like crushed diamonds; the sun was brass, and the land felt like an oven.

"How do I look, Ariel?"

"Fine, Papa."

"If'n it's Injuns," said Larke Ellen, "looking smart ain't gonna help none."

"Perhaps," said Papa, straightening his celluloid collar. Being neat and presentable was important to Papa. He always said that dignified behavior goes hand in hand with a dignified appearance.

I ran to the wagon, grabbed the Walker, and hastily loaded it. My hands were shaking. Shoving the heavy pistol in the waistband of my pants, I buttoned my jacket so Papa would not see the pistol, at least not yet.

I squinted hard, and as the riders drew near, I saw a pennant flapping. I saw yellow stripes against blue leggings; I saw hat brims soaked in sweat.

The United States cavalry slowed and lurched to a halt, and the commanding officer, nudging his horse forward, wearily saluted Papa.

"Captain Peterson, 7th Cavalry out of Fort Dragoon."

Papa introduced us all, adding, "At your service, Captain."

"You folks know where you are?"

"The Arizona Territory?" said Papa.

Captain Peterson frowned, climbed off his horse. He yanked off his leather gauntlets, stared hard at Papa, then at the rest of us, one by one. His eyes were deep green, and he seemed to disapprove of us immediately. The Captain had a lavishly waxed mustache that he tugged with his fingers, a habitual gesture. He slapped at the fine grit of grime on his blue coat. His army boots had an overlay of yellow dust; his face was windburned, his lips cracked.

"You are not far from a graveyard, sir, that's where you are."

"Excuse me?"

"Apache country, sir. This is the land of Victorio and his sister Lozen. You do not want to tussle with such savages. They will torture you men, outrage the women, and smile the whole time they are doing it. They ain't like us. They ain't Christian. You understand what I'm saying?"

"Yes, Captain, we do."

"We are not authorized to escort civilians to the fort nor to any settlements. I am sorry, but my orders are clear on that issue. We are on patrol and cannot be slowed down by civilians."

"Ariel, what is 'escort'?"

I ran forward and translated into Yiddish.

Papa replied, "We do not ask for an escort, Captain."

Peterson squinted hard, focused on Papa's beard and peyes.

"You are of the Hebrew faith, are you not?"

Papa nodded.

"I am an educated man. I recognize your Old Testament manner. Before the war I attended Harvard College, sir. For a while I considered life as a preacher. But the war changed all that."

Peterson gazed off into the mountains, into the distance. He looked like a lost man surveying the empty wastes of a raw and grand country.

The captain gave an order, and a big-bellied sergeant with a thick Irish accent barked another order. There was the creak of saddles and the jingle of bridle bits, and the two dozen troopers listlessly dismounted, gathering in the shade of some stunted cottonwoods where they gnawed on hardtack and thirstily drank from their water skins. It was at least a hundred and ten in the shade. The soldiers gaped at Rebecca and Larke Ellen; they whispered among themselves, laughed rudely and snickered.

I noticed one soldier. Something about his face, his bearing drew my attention. He was sitting alone and off to the side. He was a private, and he pushed back his hat brim and squeezed sweat from his black hair. The private gazed at me and nodded. He seemed to smile a shy smile, but I couldn't be sure. I nodded a silent greeting.

A soldier said, "Apache country."

"Why do we want it? It's some ugly country," someone shot back scornfully.

"But look at that beautiful sight," another soldier said, looking directly at Rebecca.

"Cossacks," fumed Mama. She immediately and firmly ordered Larke Ellen and Rebecca into the wagon, away from the hungry eyes of the horse soldiers.

"But it's so hot, can't we just stay under the wagon?" begged Rebecca.

"Get in the wagon where those animals can't see an inch of you. Now!"

When Mama was angry, there was no arguing with her. She was immovable. Lamenting the brutal heat, Rebecca and Larke Ellen climbed inside.

"And don't come out till those Cossacks are gone," ordered Mama.

"They're not Cossacks, Mama, they are American soldiers," said Rebecca.

"All men in uniform are Cossacks," said Mama as she dropped and laced the rear canvas tarp. The girls moaned. Now they would not catch even the slightest breeze.

Papa and I sat down with Captain Peterson. Mama boiled water. She served tea and cake.

"The men think you are Amish. They are an ignorant group. However, when it comes to fighting the Apache, I do not want fine and fancy gentlemen. If you don't mind me asking, what are you folks doing all alone, way out here?"

I gave Papa a warning look and jumped in with the simplest explanation: "We're on our way to Tombstone, Captain." I did not want Papa to tell Captain Peterson what happened back at the settlement. I certainly did not want Papa to start talking about his search for the Lamed Vovniks.

"Tombstone's a fair distance, son, nearly a hundred miles, and all of it dangerous. What do you plan to do when a party of Apache bucks comes riding after your scalps?"

"Pray?" Papa said.

Captain Peterson grinned and turned to me. "Can you fight, son? You and your pa do not look like hard men."

"We are tougher than we look."

"I'm sure that's true. The journey of immigrants to our grand land is a fearsome pilgrimage. My own people are Norwegian, and their passage was terrible. And I would be the last person to dismiss the power of prayer. Though prayer and Mr. Colt's six-shooter are a far better combination. However, let me tell you something else. Out here in the Arizona Territory, the Lord has withdrawn his divine presence."

Papa said, "That is not possible."

"Sir, I saw horror in the War of Secession, but nothing to compare with what the Apache do out here. And not just the Apache. There are white men, mixed bloods, and scalphunters, all just as low as the Apache, all making war on one another over this miserable land. I suggest you go back where you came from."

"We cannot."

"And why is that?"

"We just cannot," repeated Papa.

Captain Peterson sighed and sipped Mama's tea.

"It says in the Book that you are a stiff-necked people."

"It does. And what it really means, the deeper meaning, is that we are stubborn in our loyalty to God and the Torah," said Papa.

"That's not how I learned it."

"There are many explanations for each and every letter in the Torah. There are worlds within worlds."

Captain Peterson drained his cup of tea. "You're a pretty smart talker. But believe me, smart talk will not help if Victorio shows up. And he will. You can be sure of it. For as far as your eye can see, this is his land."

"Everywhere we go we hear about Victorio," said Papa. "Can any man be so fearsome?"

Peterson smiled. "You ever hear of Napoleon?"

"Of course."

"Well, there's nothing Napoleon knew that Victorio doesn't know a whole lot better. I once tracked him and half a dozen of his bucks over two hundred miles. They were on a raid. Never even saw their shadows. I lost half my troop to thirst, sun and sickness. He did not even have to fight me to beat me. Let me tell you something. Victorio and Lozen, together they can hammer down the gates of Rome."

"We have been in America for a little over four years. There have been many hardships. We have traveled all the way from New York, Captain, and so far we have been safe. I trust that God will continue to watch over us."

"You can trust in God all you want, sir. I, on the other hand, believe in just one thing."

"And what is that, Captain?"

"Being good and afraid of the Apache. Keeps a man alive out here."

Out of the corner of my eye, I saw the private approach Mama as she sat like a military guard at the rear of the wagon. I eased away from Papa and Captain Peterson and rushed over to Mama's side.

"You get back to your Cossack friends before I knock your head in, you dirty little sheygitz." Mama lifted a cast iron skillet; it must have weighed ten pounds.

"Please, ma'am, I'm not a sheygitz. My name is Schulman. I'm a landsman. A Jew."

Mama stared hard at the private. The heavy skillet was still held high in her hand, ready to pound his skull.

"You're a Jew?" I said.

The soldier nodded. "My parents are from Galicia. They settled in St. Louis and run a dry goods shop. Maybe you heard of it? 'Schulman's Low Priced Dry Goods.'"

"Why aren't you in the business?" said Mama, ever practical. "Why are you out here in the middle of nowhere?"

"Adventure. I wanted adventure."

Mama was astonished. "Meshugah. What kind of notion is adventure? Adventure, that's not for Jews. That's for goyim who don't have any common sense."

"I must admit, it's not what I thought it would be. The adventure wears off pretty quickly."

"Sit down," said Mama, "have a glass of tea. Adventure.

I never heard such a thing from a Jewish boy. Do you write to your mama?"

"Yes, every week."

"And what does she say?"

"She says come home. She doesn't understand that I just can't get up and leave whenever I want. If I did, that would be desertion, and I'd be shot."

"And your papa?"

"He won't write. He's too angry."

"What do you expect, with you running off and leaving the family and the business? And what does he tell the other Jews about his son, how could he possibly explain such a thing?"

"I made a mistake," said Schulman miserably. He looked like he was going to cry.

"There was a girl, right?"

He shot her a stunned look. "How did you know?"

"Young man, you think I have lived all my life on the moon? A boy runs away to the army just for adventure? No, there's always a girl involved. Rebecca, get back inside the wagon!"

Mama had eyes in the back of her head. I had to turn around to see that Rebecca had climbed out of the wagon. She was drenched in sweat, her cotton dress plastered to her skin.

"I will not," insisted Rebecca. "There is no air in there." She looked at the Jewish soldier.

"Hello, Private Schulman." Rebecca curtsied.

Schulman leaped to his feet, frantically tore his campaign hat off his head and held it close to his chest.

"H-h-hello," he stammered.

"You don't talk to my daughter."

"Oh, Mama. I heard everything. You won't let me talk to a Jewish boy?"

"He's a bum."

"Mama, why are you being so cruel?"

"It's all right," said Schulman, "I'm afraid your Mama is right. I will leave. Thank you for the tea. It's just, well, seeing Jews again. It means so much to me."

He turned to go.

"Schulman," said Mama.

"Yes?"

"You like honey cake?"

"Very much."

"So where you going so fast, you got another adventure to run off to maybe?"

Schulman told us about his life as a soldier. Mostly it was a life of endless tedium, dusty drills in the fort's quadrangle, barrack inspections by fierce sergeants, and long nights spent guarding the fort's stockades. And there were the patrols here in Apache country, three-day swings through wide areas of brutal wilderness. The soldiers eat dust, broil under the endless sun during the day, and freeze in the desert nights. Water is scarce; the food is filled with worms, and the fear of the Apache makes liquid of a soldier's stomach.

"We find tracks, signs of a raiding Apache party, but it don't mean anything, because once you find the tracks they're ten hours old, and the Apache are already fifty, sixty miles away."

"You can't catch them?" I asked.

"Let me tell you about the Apache. They only get caught when they want to be caught, and then you better watch out. It means they're already looking right down your throat. And if it comes to that, you're as good as dead. Some folks call them cowards. I don't see it that way. I call them defiant and smart. I've seen a dozen Apache braves wear down a hundred well-armed troopers. Oh, eventually we'll win, but that's only because of numbers. We're hundreds of thousands. Apache, why there can't be more than seven, eight thousand at most."

Schulman then went on to tell us about life in Fort Dragoon.

"At night the soldiers drink whiskey and gamble in saloons and go to certain kinds of well, establishments—"

"What kind of establishments?" I asked.

"Sha-shtill," snapped Mama.

A deep crimson crept into Rebecca's cheeks.

"Men are men," Larke Ellen sighed. She had finally joined our little circle.

"And the soldiers just get drunk and usually end up fighting and sometimes killing each other with knives and broken bottles."

"Nice life for a Jewish boy," said Mama.

"The other soldiers all hate me," said Schulman. "They call me coward. They say that Jews can't fight. They say that Jews are not warriors, and when it comes time to fight the Apache I'll turn yellow and run."

"How can they say such things?" cried Rebecca.

"It's not just me they're talking about. They say all Jews are cowards. They say no Jew can fight. They say all Jews know how to do is make money and cheat people."

"Such nonsense," said Mama. "If Jews are so good at business, then how come we are always so poor?"

Schulman shook his head. His eyes were bloodshot, his face gaunt. "I'll tell you this, when the time comes, when we do get into battle, I'll fight well, I'll fight bravely, I'll fight like a lion. I'll show them. I'll show them all how a Jew can fight." He knitted his eyebrows and turned to me. "In our tradition, weren't Jews great warriors?"

"Oh yes," I said, "many, many great warriors: think of Joshua, and King David, Bar Kochba, and of course the Maccabees. We fought a great rebellion against the mighty Roman Empire, and when the final battle was lost, rather than let ourselves be slaughtered or sold into slavery, a thousand men, women and children courageously committed suicide on a mountain called Masada. We were always great warriors, our generals were brilliant tacticians, and often, very often, God's angels would lead our armies into battle."

Private Schulman was silent as he strained to absorb every word that I had uttered. He seemed to grow dizzy and happy.

"On purpose you'll risk your life?" said Mama, breaking the silence.

"Of course," snapped Rebecca. "Private Schulman wants to show them. You want to prove to them how brave a Jew can be, right?"

"Yes, yes, I most certainly do. And call me Max."

"And I am Rebecca."

Max gazed at Rebecca for a long, long moment. Rebecca gazed at Max for a long, long moment. Their eyes were locked and the significance was not lost on Mama. Her lips compressed with grim reserve.

Captain Peterson and his troopers camped a hundred yards away near a powder-dry arroyo. They would resume their patrol the next day.

The captain told Papa that he had studied Latin, Greek and Hebrew back in Harvard College. He recited some biblical Hebrew for us. Papa and I could barely understand a word he said. Harvard may be a big and fancy college, but they don't know anything about Hebrew. However, Captain Peterson seemed so proud of his learning that we did not want to shatter his illusions, and we assured him that his knowledge was impressive. He smiled hugely, tugged the edges of his mustache and again begged us to return to the settlement where we had come from or risk losing our scalps to Victorio.

The sun made a last bloody splash.

❧

Chapter 3

—· Rebecca Has an Admirer ·—

In the middle of the night, I heard the soft crunch of footsteps against soil turned to crumbled powder by the blistering sun. I was sleeping under the wagon, and I saw a shadow fleeing across the flats, past the arroyo.

I made a wide circle round the cavalry pickets and heard them whispering before I saw them.

He said, "I wasn't sure you would come."

"I shouldn't, I really shouldn't," she replied in a whisper.

"Then why?"

"You seem...."

"What?"

"Nice."

As my eyes adjusted to the gloom, I could see Rebecca's large dark eyes; they appeared like onyx in the moonlight. Her motions and expressions gradually came into focus; it was as if my sister radiated her own celestial light.

"Max?"

"Yes, Rebecca?"

"Nothing...."

"No, what is it?"

"Tell me about the girl." She picked absently, coquettishly, at the long curls of dark hair that fell across her breast. Her ringlets gleamed like wild metal turnings. She was wearing one of her best dresses, a gingham frock with a powder blue bow at the waist. I could smell the vanilla extract that she had dabbed behind each ear.

"What girl?"

"The girl back in St. Louis. The girl Mama talked about."

"Her parents owned a fabric store. They were well off, and everyone thought it would be a good shidduch."

"And you didn't?"

"No. I met her. I tried. But we didn't hit it off; we really didn't have anything to talk about. How could I marry her?"

"No romance."

"No nothing."

"So you ran away."

"The pressure was terrible."

"I know what that's like."

"Do you?"

"Of course." Rebecca hesitated, then: "Max?"

"What?"

"How much longer are you going to be a soldier?"

"Another year."

"Oh, God."

"Why?"

"Why, like Mama said, it's no life for a Jewish boy."

That's when I made a noise. A small sneeze, a tiny achoo. Abruptly, Rebecca had me by the neck and shoulder; she was twisting my arm, hissing in my ear.

"You little monster, did Mama send you to spy on me?"

"No, no," I cried.

"I ought to spank you. What did you hear?"

"Nothing."

"Liar."

"Everything."

"If you tell Mama, I'll kill you. Do you hear me? I'll kill you."

"Rebecca," said Max, "don't."

My sister's voice lifted dangerously. "You don't understand, Max. Mama will lock me up forever. You don't know her. You don't know them. If they find out about this, about us…"

"Us?" said Max, shocked.

"But Max," she said, "I thought, I thought…."

"What, what did you think?"

Rebecca's whole body trembled and finally shook uncontrollably. She sank to the ground and hugged her knees. She looked as if she were made of wax and had moved too close to a flame. No one moved; we were still; all of us seemed rooted in place, afraid even to breathe.

"I'd better go back," said Max.

Rebecca looked at him. Her eyes flashed silver, hard and angry. He could not meet her gaze, and he dropped his head.

"Go back, what do you mean?"

"I don't want to cause trouble, Rebecca."

Rebecca stiffened like a violin string. She let the stillness hang for a moment, then: "I *want* you to cause trouble," she said. Her voice was harsh. "I don't give up when I don't get what I want."

Max's shoulders sagged; he retreated and appeared to me like a frightened animal. Rebecca's eyes were fixed on him, cool and contemptuous.

"I think maybe the soldiers were right about you, Max."

"Right? I don't understand. Right about what?"

"What do you think, soldier boy?"

Rebecca was now brusque, almost indifferent.

"About you being a coward."

Max flinched, as if punched in the stomach. Here was a man who was not at all prepared for Rebecca's passionate and demanding nature. I tried to catch Rebecca's eye, to give her a look begging her to have some sympathy for poor Private Schulman. But her eyes were fixed on the nervous soldier, nailing him with a merciless challenge to be the man she wanted him to be: a knight in shining armor.

I never realized how much of Mama there was in Rebecca. I was seeing it, really seeing it, for the first time. A vague corner of my mind was suddenly alerted and alive.

"I'd better get back before the pickets come looking for me," he said feebly.

Rebecca said nothing. She just looked at him. A dust devil whirled in the shape of a tornado out in the desert.

Max turned away, slipped back to his lines and camp. In a moment, he was absorbed by the night. Rebecca mopped her eyes with the heel of her hand.

"Are you crying, Rebecca?"

Her answer was a while in coming. "No, it's just sand in my eyes."

There was a small rush of night wind around us. Rebecca shivered and hugged herself.

"I'm sorry," I said.

"Forget it," she murmured bleakly. "Anyway, he's not worth it."

"Rebecca?"

"Yes?"

"What is it you want?"

"There is no way you could ever understand."

"You think I'm stupid?"

"No, you are smart, terribly smart, but you are also very young."

"What do you want, Rebecca? I want to understand, I really do."

She fixed her gaze on me. Her face looked like a shield. She was a coiled spring of unmet needs.

"I want to attend an ice-cream social," she said quietly, evenly. She gathered herself, then stood up, looked down at me and shook her head slowly from side to side in a display of pity.

"Poor little boy."

Silent, I looked up at her, a burning sensation creeping behind my eyes.

She studied my expression and chuckled.

"Ariel, you look like a tongue-tied actor."

"I just don't know what to say."

"I knew you wouldn't understand."

Rebecca made her way back to the wagon. I sat on the ground and watched the sun rise. It was a bitter red disk.

◎ ◎ ◎

In the morning, Captain Peterson made a strange request of Papa. He asked Papa to act as chaplain for the troopers, to say a prayer, a true "Old Testament entreaty."

"Something to stiffen the boys' spines for an encounter with the Apache," said Peterson.

Papa tried to get out of it, politely tried to convince Peterson that the Christian soldiers would resent the prayer of a Jewish rabbi. However, Peterson insisted that the soldiers would appreciate what they were ordered to appreciate. Besides, added Peterson, it was Papa's duty as a new American citizen to help strengthen the morale of U.S. soldiers, especially soldiers going up against the fearsome Apache. Finally, Papa relented.

He put on his fine frock coat, Mama knotted his silk tie, and I polished his boots with lampblack.

The horse soldiers were mustered in line. "Company 'ten-shun!'" roared the big-bellied sergeant.

The troopers gathered, at first silent, then muttering among themselves. Men and horses grew impatient and short-tempered as Papa leafed through his books, trying to decide what to recite. I gazed at Private Max Schulman. He had trouble maintaining eye contact and looked past me, searching for Rebecca, but she had not come out of the wagon. Finally, Max's eyes, sad, unsure and embarrassed, fixed themselves to a spot in the far distance, past the sweeping desert, to the heroic Dragoon Mountains.

"Ah, this one," Papa finally murmured. Papa chanted. His voice ascended majestically, floating in the wilderness with great dignity.

Papa recited in Hebrew, and I translated into English. At first, the cavalry soldiers looked bored and anxious to ride off, but soon, Papa's intense reading broke through their indifference. They were staring at Papa, all eyes fixed on him as if hypnotized, and the Prophet Joel's exalted words gripped their hearts and minds.

> *Announce this among the nations; prepare for war; arouse the mighty; let all the soldiers approach and ascend. Beat your plowshares into swords and your pruning forks into spears; the weak shall say, I am strong.*

As the soldiers rode off, Max Schulman turned in his saddle, hoping for a parting glance of Rebecca, but my sister did not climb out of the wagon until Max and all the other horse soldiers were just specks in the landscape.

Chapter 4

—· Queen of the Desert ·—

An hour later, just as we were about to break camp, a fountain of dust floated up from a nearby arroyo. The powder thickened, and a horseman appeared on the rise, as if coming up from the depths.

It was a woman.

She rode steadily onward with a huge rifle across her thighs. Her horse was white and very tall, with flaring nostrils and eyes as wide as saucers.

"Lord, that's a devil Apache woman," Larke Ellen said. She held tight to her baby.

But the rider was not a woman. She was a *girl*, an Indian girl, not much older than me. She had skin like burnished mahogany. Her hair was bluish-black and woven into two long braids, thick as whip handles, which were neatly tucked into the belt at her waist. The Apache girl wore a soft white buckskin shirt and a long calico dress. Her moccasins had the distinctive upturned toe of the Apache Indians.

"Papa, do something," Mama pleaded.

But Papa was davening the morning prayer, Shacharis. Papa had donned his tefillin, phylacteries, and he wore his tallis, his prayer shawl, draped over his head.

He swayed to and fro. He did not see the Apache girl. He did not see the barren Arizona desert. He did not hear Mama's cry. He was in dialogue with God.

The girl rider focused her gaze on Papa, slowly drinking him in. Her eyes were like burning coals. She urged her horse forward; the horse shied momentarily, then stepped forward and circled Papa, round and round. She studied his face, considered his lips as they mouthed the sacred prayers. At that moment the landscape changed; it was as if the world had become transformed into something entirely different. The sun blazed down through the morning fog and mirrored over the sparkling stream. Shadows fell deeper black behind every granite rock in the distant canyons. The whine, stab, and itch of mosquitoes irritated Papa not at all.

Rebecca cowered under the wagon. I stood rooted to the spot, feeling the Walker pistol in the waistband of my pants, feeling its deadly weight; aware of the smooth oiled steel, the fully automatic action, a machine for killing. My hand moved towards the pistol. Slowly. Ever so slowly.

The Apache girl frowned and adjusted a formidable belt of cartridges that was buckled across her chest. She turned her gaze towards me.

My hand froze. Did she see the gun? Did she know? Was I about to die? Were we all about to die?

"Does this man make medicine?" she asked.

I tried to answer, but no words came out of my mouth. I was so scared that my throat had tightened and closed as if a cork had been shoved into my mouth.

"What kind of medicine?" the Apache girl said.

Her tone was surprisingly soft. Like a musical note.

Finally, I found my voice. "My father is a holy man," I said.

"Another missionary?" she said. This time her tone was flat and edged with anger. In one fluid motion, her hand dropped a slack rein, glided to her belt, and swung a big pistol, a Colt Dragoon, out from her body, levered the hammer, and pointed it at me, at Papa, at all of us. Her horse shied and whinnied.

"No. Oh, no," I exclaimed. "We are Jews."

She looked confused. "Not Christians?" She reined her horse under control by instinct with the tips of her toes. I felt my knees and ankles shaking. My hands tingled.

"We are not Christians, not missionaries."

The Indian girl kept her silence for a moment. If she moved, I decided, I would yank the Walker and shoot at her as many times as I could and hope to God that I hit her before she killed any of us. All I heard was the stream making its gentle, downhill music, as cool water washed across limestone pebbles. Abruptly, another sound mushroomed inside my head: the click of her pistol—dry and sharp—as she expertly eased down the hammer. She shoved the pistol back into her belt. Well oiled, the Colt

Dragoon flashed in the morning light; the muzzle and cylinder gleamed like polished gems.

"What are those boxes the old man wears? What is the leather around his arm and head?"

"Tefillin," I said. "It is worn for the morning prayer by the Jewish people."

"And the striped blanket?"

"It's a tallis, a holy garment."

Her lips moved. She was repeating the words tallis and tefillin, memorizing the strange new sounds. Nothing could hide the intelligence, or the ferocity, in her eyes.

"Who do you worship?" she asked.

"God."

"Which God?"

"There is only one God."

Her black eyes leapt out at me. Then once again she glanced over at Papa, who was still swaying back and forth.

"What does the bearded one ask for? Rain? Crops? Horses? Many children?"

"He asks for protection. He begs for mercy. He praises God and proclaims him to be the one God."

She thought this over for a long moment. There was a long, wicked knife with a horn handle in a leather sheath dangling from her belt.

"Can he heal the sick?"

"Absolutely."

Mama shot me a wary look.

"He has done this before?" she asked.

"A child was sick, dying, and Papa prayed all night by the child's bed. The doctor said the child would be dead by morning. But when the sun rose, so did the child."

"You saw this?"

"I was the child."

"Ussen is the one God," she said calmly.

Everybody said that the Apache spend all their time stealing horses, murdering settlers, and kidnapping children. But here I was, meeting my very first Apache, and we were talking about God. As Papa said, America is a wondrous land.

"Who are you?" she asked me.

Standing tall and squaring my shoulders, I said with reckless courage, "I am the Hebrew Kid, Terror of the Arizona Territory." I fear that my voice quavered.

She laughed. Her laughter chimed clear and crystal, like a bell in the immense wilderness. Her teeth were very even and white, immaculate as the ivory keys of a piano.

"And I am Lozen, sister of Victorio, Mimbres Apache."

She nudged her horse with the toe of her moccasin and galloped away. Dust spurted from the hooves of the horse.

Lozen crossed my vision like a moon. Nothing seemed to touch her.

I stood rooted to the spot, watching Lozen, the Apache maiden, ride off into the desert. In a moment she was just a mote in the eye, a speck moving in the shimmering distance. And then she was gone. Like a ghost, she seemed to merge into the desolate landscape. The desert became deathly still.

I did not know it then, but I had just met one of the most fearsome warriors of the Apache nation. And Lozen, sister of the great warrior Victorio, would forever change the course of my life.

"Goddle mighty. I seen all the fires of hell rise up in that evil girl's eyes," said Larke Ellen. She passed the water bag to me and watched gravely as I drank. It took me a moment to catch my breath.

'Why ain't you scared?" she asked.

"I am."

"It don't seem like it."

What could I say? There was something about Lozen that fired my imagination. She was like some desert princess, proud and courageous. I thought of the prophetess Devorah leading a Jewish army into battle against the Canaanites. I thought of Yael, another brave woman, who slew the evil King Sisera. Of course, there was something savage and awful about Lozen. It was startling to be confronted by such a young girl armed with pistol, rifle and twin ammunition bandoleers crossed over her chest. From the moment I set eyes on the Apache maiden, I knew there was something about her that was untamed and untamable.

When Papa finished praying, Mama and Rebecca pounced on him and blurted out their tale of the fearsome Apache maiden. Papa listened. He stroked his cheeks; his beard appeared a black whirlwind devouring the steep rise of his sharp cheekbones. Papa nodded his head. He turned to me.

"Ariel, what do you make of this girl?"

"A lion, Papa."

Rebecca threw up her hands. "A savage. A half-naked savage."

"Rebecca, she was dressed very modestly," I said reasonably. "Her arms were covered, and so were her legs."

"Has my family gone completely meshugah?" Mama thundered. "You are arguing over what the Indian was wearing. I'll tell you what she was wearing: a gun, a very big gun, and a knife, almost as big."

"But she didn't use them," said Papa thoughtfully.

Larke Ellen spoke: "She's Victorio's sister. Are you folks aware of how many white folks that Victorio's killed? Not to mention greasers."

"Greasers?" said Papa. "What means greasers?"

"Mexicans," I explained.

"Papa," cried Mama, "let us get out of here while we are still alive. Please."

Papa turned and looked out at the desert. The paloverde trees were in full golden bloom, and the cactus was crowned with white flowers. Beside the river, the mesquites and cottonwoods flourished, and the Dragoon Mountains shone rosy pink and lavender in the late morning sun. Papa smiled.

"Mama," said Rebecca, "Papa's smiling."

"I know," said Mama, taking Rebecca by the hand.

"Why is Papa smiling?"

"Papa, why are you smiling?"

Papa said nothing.

"Ariel, why is he smiling?" Mama demanded to know.

I looked at Papa's beaming face, and I thought that perhaps I understood his strange joy.

"Papa smiles because we are still alive. If the Apache girl had meant to kill us she would have. Yes, Papa?"

Papa brushed his hand over my cheek. He kept his eyes fixed on the distant mountains.

"We are safe," he finally said. "The Apache girl will not harm us."

Mama threw up her hands in disgust. Rebecca stamped her feet in anger. Larke Ellen observed us with round-eyed wonder.

And I thought to myself: the great Victorio also will not harm us?

All through the Arizona and New Mexico territories, the Apache warrior's name sent children crying into their mothers' arms, made grown men quake with fear, caused pregnant women to lose their babies.

They say that no man who fought against Victorio ever lived to tell about it. The army scouts who drifted through the settlements spoke of tracking Victorio and his warriors for weeks at a time but never seeing so much as his shadow. With just a handful of braves, Victorio moved like the wind and struck like a hammer. His hatred for the white man was legendary. Yes, Victorio well remembered how his leader, the great Mangas Coloradas, was brutally whipped and then murdered by government soldiers.

It seemed that most everyone in the territory felt relieved or just plain indifferent to Mangas Coloradas' unjust end. But Papa sadly shook his head and said that even war has rules. He insisted that the Torah forbade mutilation and torture. "We are made in God's image," Papa taught, "and it is a negation of this belief to mutilate the flesh of a human being, even your most bitter enemy."

Papa was scared of the Apache, but he also felt sorry for them. "Imagine it like this," he said to me; "as we feel about Cossacks, the Apache feels about the white men."

"But," I countered, "doesn't the white man see the Apache as the Cossack?"

"Yes, yes," agreed Papa with a sigh, "and we Jews are in the middle."

We felt safe, and once again we set out to leave camp. When no one was looking, I hid the pistol in the back of the wagon. "Hopefully," said Rebecca, "we will never see that savage Apache girl again."

But less than an hour later Lozen returned; she rode into camp with the fury of an avenging angel.

Chapter 5
—· Medicine or Prayer ·—

The Apache Maiden was riding hard; her pony was lathered in sweat, and its legs were trembling from exhaustion. Holding out her leather whip towards Papa, she said, "My medicine is not working."

"Excuse?" said Papa.

Lozen nudged her horse towards Papa. "Apache is sick. All medicine men have tried and failed. Now you must come and pray to your God. You must save his life."

"And if I don't?" asked Papa.

Lozen drew her Colt Dragoon, cocked the hammer and pointed the pistol at Papa.

"I see."

"Hebrew Kid says you can heal by talking to God."

Frowning, Papa shot me a disapproving look. I shrugged feebly.

"Thank you, Ariel," said Papa with cold anger.

"Come, come," said Lozen. She threw out her hand, motioned Papa to ride double with her. Papa hesitated.

"Papa can't ride," I explained. "He falls off horses. He has to ride on the wagon." Lozen turned the gun on me.

"Just the holy man comes to Apache camp," said Lozen.

"No," I said. "All of us. We can't stay here alone. We won't be separated. We're a family."

"Just the Holy Man." She was adamant.

I stared at the barrel of the gun. It seemed limitless, enormous, as if I could hop onto the barrel and slide along for miles and miles. I glanced back at Lozen, anxious that fear was showing on my face.

"Papa won't go without me," I insisted. "And where I go, the rest of the family goes. And if you shoot any of us, your Apache will surely die."

Our eyes met and dueled for a long moment. My heart was drumming in my chest, crawling into my throat, and her finger was pale, like a snowflake on the trigger. Lozen eased the hammer down and shoved the Dragoon back into her belt.

"Hurry. No stopping for anything."

As the wagon rattled and shook along, I looked at Mama and Papa, Rebecca and Larke Ellen; they were all seized with fear.

◉ ◉ ◉

For five grueling hours, we followed a winding path into thin air. The land was stark except for balls of tumbleweed and the purple mountains in the distance. Rattlesnakes squirmed in the sagebrush; tarantulas crawled over pale rock faces. Abruptly, we hit a flat plateau. There were a dozen dome-shaped wickiups with conical tops. They were made of a framework of poles and limbs tied together, covered over with a thatch of bear grass, brush, and yucca leaves. They were all open at the top, and thin wisps of smoke snaked into the darkening sky. The doorways were low openings over which pieces of skin were stretched. All the doorways faced east.

I was driving the creaking wagon, Mama on one side of me, Papa on the other. Larke Ellen and Rebecca cowered in the back. Suspicious Apache braves watched as we drove into their camp. Half-naked children, terrified of the white-eyes, cowered behind their mothers' wide skirts. Vicious dogs, all ribs and running pink sores, barked, growled furiously and lunged at the wagon wheels.

"I got me a two-shot Derringer," said Larke Ellen. "If one of them bucks tries to have me as his wife, I'll take my own life."

"I don't think I'd have the courage," said Rebecca.

"That's all right, I'll do you first," said Larke Ellen.

"Thank you."

"You're welcome."

"Sha-shtill," said Mama. "Nobody commits suicide without my permission, is that understood?"

"Yes, Mama."

"That goes for you too, Larke Ellen. You have a baby to think of. You want your baby to be an orphan? Are you that selfish?"

"I wasn't thinking."

"That's the problem with this generation, they never think."

◎ ◎ ◎

Lozen ushered Papa and me into one of the wickiups. It took a second for my eyes to adjust to the gloom. Through a veil of smoke, I saw a young boy stretched out on a bed of threadbare blankets, his chest rising up and down ever so slowly. Even from a few paces away, I could hear his labored breathing. By his side, a sturdy-looking man with long black hair sat cross-legged staring at the child's face. On the man's wrist, I noticed a bracelet made of turquoise stones; as I drew closer I saw that on each stone was carved a tiny animal: a deer, a mountain lion, a horse. He said something to Lozen in their language. Lozen answered. He looked at Papa. Rigidly, Papa stood in the entrance, his siddur in his hands. The man stood up. He was barrel-chested and of small stature. Yet something about his presence, an air of steely competence, of quiet menace, made him vaguely intimidating. A blue bandanna was wrapped round his forehead. He spoke the guttural Apache language; his words flew; his eyes fixed on me, on Papa, and then he was gone. He seemed a master of this severe Apache world.

"He says to save his nephew; he has only fifteen summers, and someday he will be a great warrior," said Lozen.

"That was Victorio, wasn't it?" I said.

Lozen nodded, just once, a stately inclination of her head.
I swallowed a dry lump.

Papa insisted that Lozen wait outside for a few moments.
He kneeled by the Apache boy, pressed his ear to the
rasping chest and listened for a minute or two.

"What is it, Papa?"

"Sshh...."

I waited.

"There is congestion in the lungs."

"And?"

"Look how the poor boy is sweating, the shivering, and
feel his head."

When I pressed the palm of my hand to the boy's
forehead, his skin felt hot as a skillet.

"I would say he probably has a touch of malaria," said
Papa.

"That's bad, isn't it?"

"It is not good."

"So praying might not help."

"On the other hand, praying might very well help.
Where would the Jewish people be without prayer, Ariel?
Go tell Mama to get busy cooking the soup."

"The soup?"

"Mama will know."

I started to go outside.

"And Ariel?"

"Yes, Papa?"

"Next time, don't be so fast to tell people that your
father can cure the sick."

I already regretted what I had told Lozen. "I'm sorry, Papa," I said. "I was just trying to…"

"I know what you were trying to do. Remember, sometimes words are like glass that breaks in your mouth. Tell Mama to prepare the soup. Quickly."

Outside, I ran to the wagon, where Mama was surrounded by a crescent of Apache women and little girls.

Mama was saying, "And these are my Shabbos candle-sticks. I put in the candles here," Mama demonstrated how she slotted the candles, "and then light the match and say the bracha, the prayer, and then poof, time becomes holy, and from sundown to sundown we do not work."

The Apache women and girls fell into frenzied discussion, examined Mama's candlesticks. They showered her with questions, all in Apache. It was chaotic. As I drew closer, I saw that Lozen was in the center, translating, trying to bring some semblance of order to Mama's presentation.

"What does Papa think?" Mama murmured.

"Malaria," I whispered.

"Oy vey."

"Papa says to make the soup."

"The soup."

"He says you'll know."

Mama nodded her head, turned to Lozen and said, "Lozen, it works like this: the rabbi prays and I make a potion, a special potion for the boy to drink. Hopefully this will heal him."

"You are a witch?"

Mama's face turned deep pink. She exploded. "God forbid!" Mama spit three times to avoid the evil eye. "I'm just a very special cook. I make a fine broth filled with herbs from the old country, and hopefully this will help your sick boy. There is no witchcraft! Jewish women do not make dark magic. I'll have you know that I come from a family of great scholars. My father was a great rabbi, and his father was a great rabbi, and all the way back to Mt. Sinai. So you be careful who you call a witch. Let me tell you something, you might scare the goyim with your whoops and hollers and guns and knives, but to me you're just a little shicksah pisher. And a little advice, maidel: you should spend a bit more time on your looks; you got nice features. Good strong bones, and your hair, it's gorgeous, if a bit shmutzik. You think a man is going to want to marry a wild girl? You should be thinking about a shidduch, not riding around like you're on the warpath!"

Mama was practically shouting. Lozen nodded mutely. Clearly, she didn't understand why Mama was so upset about being labeled a witch. In fact, she did not comprehend most of what Mama was shouting. Mama's English was heavily accented and with so much Yiddish thrown in, well, we were lucky that Lozen did not grasp enough to be offended.

Mama ordered Lozen to build a cooking fire right outside the sick boy's wickiup.

This Lozen did understand. "White-eyes should not order Apache to build fire," Lozen said with pained dignity.

"Mameleh, you want the boy to get better or you want to argue? I figure you can build a fire a bit faster than we can, and we have to move quickly because you have a very sick boy in there. So, what's it to be?"

Lozen stomped away and started building a fire in front of the wickiup. Mama climbed into the wagon and, with Rebecca by her side, mixed the ingredients for the broth. Larke Ellen was still huddled in the back of the wagon, clutching her Derringer. I joined Lozen and helped her build the fire.

"Your mother, are you sure she is not a witch?" Lozen asked.

"Positive. Witchcraft is forbidden by our laws."

"Ours too."

"My mother is just...."

"What?"

"She's just... Mama."

"She is just like an Apache mother. Very strong."

I smiled. Yes, that's my Mama.

"Will the holy man's prayers be able to help?"

"I hope so."

"The story you told me, was it true?"

"Of course."

"So your God always listens to your prayers?"

Always, I thought, was a dangerous word. "Let me tell you another story. There was a woman who had just been married. She became ill on her wedding night. The doctor gave up hope. He could do nothing but watch her die.

My father was called in to pray. Papa prayed all night. He prayed like I've never seen him pray before. His face was shining, and I know, I just know that God was listening to him."

"And?"

"And in the morning the bride died."

"So God did not answer your father's prayers?"

"No, Lozen, that's where you're wrong. You see, God *did* answer Papa's prayers."

She looked at me, searching my face, trying to understand.

"God said no," I explained.

◎ ◎ ◎

Mama stirred the heavy iron kettle; the steam rose, and the fragrant odor of the broth filled my head like the rarest of perfumes. The whole village gathered round and watched as Mama added tiny pinches of various ingredients. Every so often she would sip and taste the broth, then add another ingredient. The older Apache women murmured among themselves as they thoughtfully chewed plugs of tobacco or smoked cigars. The Apache men remained separate, gazing skeptically at the whole affair. Victorio was nowhere in sight. Inside the wickiup, Papa recited psalms and every once in a while leaned over and listened to the boy's rattling chest.

Darkness came, and Mama was satisfied that the broth

was finished. She unfolded a slip of paper and poured in some powder, the last ingredient, and then I lugged the heavy kettle into the wickiup. Lozen propped the Apache boy's head up on her lap, and Mama spooned the broth between his pale lips. At first, the soup just dribbled down his chin, but after a few words of encouragement from Lozen, the boy managed to swallow a few spoonfuls, and then some more. His eyes opened, and for the first time, he saw us, and there was real fear in his eyes. He whispered something, and Lozen answered soothingly. But when we tried to feed him more soup, he clamped his lips shut and refused.

"What did he say?" I asked.

"He thinks you are devils trying to poison him," said Lozen.

"Tell him we are angels, and we are feeding him holy food," I said.

Papa shot me a frustrated look. Mama groaned. She was ready to pry the boy's mouth open and pour the broth down his throat. To refuse Mama's food was a major insult. Lozen whispered into the sick boy's ear. His eyes roamed over our faces, and after a moment he relaxed and sipped the soup. He barely had enough strength to swallow.

During the next hour, the boy's fever rose and the sweat dripped off him. I placed cool, damp rags over his forehead. Papa prayed, uneasy under Lozen's gaze. I looked questioningly at Mama, wondering why the Apache youth was getting worse.

"What's happening to him, Mama?"

Mama gave a slow shrug, and before she could answer, Lozen touched the patient's feverish forehead, then motioned me to step outside.

"Your medicine is not working."

"You must be patient."

"Is your God saying no?"

"I don't know."

"If the boy dies, so will the holy man," said Lozen with chilling nonchalance.

I looked into the bottomless depths of her eyes. My mouth was washed in the sour taste of bile. Hopelessness yawned at my feet.

"That's not right."

"It is how it is," said Lozen.

A brilliant half-moon rose over the hills, spilling light across the jagged peaks and sending a drenching silver light into the Apache camp. The wickiups glimmered as the wind brushed them into sinuous patterns. Black nighthawks swooped across the moon's bright face. Far away, a wolf howled a cry of despair.

◎   ◎   ◎

I jerked awake and opened my eyes to the morning light. When did I fall asleep? The last thing I remembered was sitting beside Lozen and taking turns wiping the cold sweat from the sick boy's forehead.

Sitting cross-legged, Lozen held the boy's hand. The Apache maiden was sobbing, silvery tears cutting thick channels down her face. The boy was dead.

✿

Chapter 6
—· Will I Have a Bar Mitzvah? ·—

This is the end, I thought to myself; the boy is dead, and now the Apache will kill us. And it was my fault. I was the one who bragged that Papa was a great healer. I was the one who claimed that God listened to Papa. I was responsible for this terrible fate.

Lozen looked at me. Her eyes were like black diamonds.

"Lozen, I'm sorry, so sorry. But please try and understand, Papa did his best, and so did Mama, and it's just not our fault."

"The holy man is responsible," she insisted.

I swallowed hard and stared at Lozen's tear-drenched face, at the revolver in her belt. What could I do against this fearsome girl? What chance did we have trapped inside an Apache camp? None; we were as good as dead.

And then the Apache boy sighed and whispered. He was breathing. He was alive. It was incredible, a miracle. I practically leaped to Lozen's side and touched the boy's forehead. His skin was dry as paper, cool to the touch. His fever was gone, and there was a blush of color in his cheeks.

"Oh my God," I said.

"The holy man makes powerful medicine," said Lozen.

I could only nod.

"Do you still say that your father is not responsible?"

I said nothing, and Lozen said, "If the boy had died, the holy man would not be responsible. But the boy is alive, and so the holy man is responsible. Is that how it is?" Lozen smiled.

I mulled this over. "I'm glad that he's better. That's what matters."

"Victorio says that you must stay until boy is up and all better. Victorio wants the holy man's prayers, wants your mother's healing soup. Agreed?"

"Do we have a choice?"

A shake of the head.

I stood up to leave.

"Thank you," she said, "thank you." I looked at her and thought to myself that the Apache maiden had a face of uncomplicated honesty.

Outside I found Mama enthusiastically bustling about, brewing more soup. She was humming a Yiddish folk song. Several old Apache women helped stir the cauldron and began to hum along with Mama. The atmosphere in the camp was wholly different now that the boy was regaining his health. Several young Apache girls were gathered around Rebecca and Larke Ellen. They watched as Rebecca displayed some of her clothing. There was a ruffled petticoat, a thin white chemise, a lace collar, wool stockings, a gingham sun-bonnet and two shirtwaists with leg-o-mutton sleeves. Rebecca was a gifted seamstress. She made all her own clothing. Her linen and cotton items went from hand to hand. The Apache girls appreciatively caressed the fine fabric. Their fascination turned to confusion when they came across Rebecca's whale-bone corset. The Apache women pelted Rebecca and Larke Ellen with questions about this strange garment.

"We wear this to make our waists nice and narrow," explained Rebecca. The Apache women exchanged questioning looks. "It's what men like," said Rebecca, "little waists, wide hips, proud bosom, and a generous tushy."

Lozen asked: "What is tushy?"

An Apache woman awkwardly slipped the stiff corset over her soft, butternut-brown deerskin shift. Larke Ellen hooked the eyelets closed and knotted the laces in the back. The Apache woman abruptly sucked in her stomach and panted vigorously, fighting to draw breath into her lungs. Everyone laughed.

I ran to Mama.

"You did it," I cried, "you and Papa saved the Apache boy. It's a miracle, a true miracle."

Mama shrugged and under her breath remarked, "Miracles shmiracles. I put sulphur and quinine into the broth. It's the best medicine for malaria."

"You gave him medicine?"

"That's what you do when someone is sick."

"So we tricked them."

Mama's eyebrow climbed. "No, using medicine is no trick. It's just common sense."

"I don't think they'd see it that way."

Mama brushed aside my thought. "Maybe, but what counts is that the boy is getting better, and we will be able to get out of here alive."

I nodded my agreement, but in my heart, I was uncomfortable, and I told Papa what I was feeling.

"Who's to say what made the boy better? Perhaps it was praying, perhaps it was the soup, and maybe it was the medicine. Do you know what I think, Ariel?"

"What, Papa?"

"I think it was the medicine and our prayers, working in combination. Do not forget, the Torah teaches us not to rely on miracles. We are made in God's image, endowed with the ability to use our brains. He does not want us to be passive vessels who beg Him to do everything for us."

I was relieved, but it was a sad joy, for I had truly believed that Papa had performed a miracle.

"Papa?"

"Yes, my son."

"What about my bar mitzvah? It's the Shabbos after next. What are you going to do about it?"

Papa searched my eyes and said, "If I knew, I would be a prophet. But I don't know, Ariel. It is hard to plan when Lozen holds us captive." He paused a moment. "You look angry, Ariel."

I avoided his eyes. I knew that Papa could read my every emotion. He put an arm over my shoulder and we walked a few paces. "Let us take your bar mitzvah one step at a time, Ariel."

"What's the first step, Papa?"

Looking grim, Papa said, "Staying alive here among the Apache."

Chapter 7

—· Knife in the Sand ·—

The next morning, Lozen ordered me to mount one of the tribe's ponies. I asked where she was taking me, but she just placed the reins in my hands and ordered me to follow her. Papa stepped in front of Lozen's horse and said, "Where are you taking my son? Will Ariel be safe?"

Lozen told Papa not to be such an old woman; to stay with the sick boy, make sure that he continued to get well.

"It's okay, Papa," I said. "I'll be fine."

We rode for several hours. I had some of Mama's kugel with me and shared it with Lozen. She smiled at the taste and said it was the best food she had ever eaten. Lozen wanted to know more about the tribe of the Jews. How were we different from the white man? Did we have missionaries? How many of us were there? Were we as numerous as the white man? Who were our enemies? Who were our friends? She plied me with questions, and I answered as best as I could. She was an inquisitive girl, and after a while I felt comfortable with her. The fear that

I had felt in her presence gradually diminished, and soon for each question she asked about the Jews, I asked her one about the Apache. When the sun was at its zenith, a brilliant burning splotch of gold, Lozen yanked on the reins and hopped off her horse.

Lozen crouched on one knee and examined the dusty tracks. She pulled the stag handled knife from her belt, wiped the blade clean with the hem of her deerskin skirt, and then, with a swift thrust, drove the blade into the earth. She left it there a moment, quivering slightly. Next Lozen leaned over, opened her mouth and clamped down on the head of the knife. She was listening for hoof beats. Her teeth picked up the vibrations through the blade in the ground. Slowly, her eyes lifted, following the sign forward along the ground, then sweeping past the flaming yellow and red rock spires of the nearby hills. A scalding whisper of wind carried gritty scarlet powder across my face.

"They are ahead of us, over that rise," said Lozen.

"Who is?"

"The men we are following."

"I thought we were just riding and talking."

Lozen smiled. I realized that she had fooled me. We weren't just casually riding and learning about one another. No, Lozen was tracking a group of horsemen the whole time. I was too green, too naïve to realize it.

Who was she following? Lozen said nothing, but I knew that the Apache were always at war with the other tribes of the Arizona Territory, the Tonkawa and the Pima.

An hour later, we left our horses at the foot of a rise and in silence climbed a low ridge. Down in a draw, Lozen found what she was looking for.

Captain Peterson and his cavalry were camped below.

Even from high above the soldiers, I was able to pick out Private Schulman. Lozen counted soldiers, made note of their weapons and supplies.

When we retreated to our horses, I asked Lozen why she was following the American soldiers.

"Scouting for my brother," she said.

"Why?"

Lozen fixed me with her dark gaze. She said nothing, but her silence was in itself an answer, and it sent a chill deep into my stomach.

"Lozen," I said, "you can't attack them."

"Why not?"

"They're not doing anything to you. Why can't you just leave them alone?"

"They are here to hunt and kill us."

"Don't, please."

"Why do you care?"

"There's no reason to attack them. They can't find you. You can avoid killing them. You can avoid a battle entirely."

"We are at war with the soldiers, with the white-eyes."

"One of the soldiers is a friend."

"He is a white-eye."

"He's a Jew, a member of my tribe."

"You want us to spare one man? Point him out, we will try."

"I want you to spare all of them."

"Why?"

"Because it's wrong to kill them."

"They would kill me if they could."

"Maybe."

"Not maybe, Ariel. They have sworn to kill every Apache."

"We helped you, Lozen. We did what you asked. Now you can do what I ask. It is only fair."

"You mean because your father saved the Apache boy?"

"Yes."

"But that is just one life. You ask too much."

"I'm not asking, I'm begging you to spare their lives."

She continued to stare at me. She knelt on one knee and traced patterns on the ground. Her horse shuffled and threw its head. She quieted the animal down by stroking its massive head and whispering into its ear.

"It is not my decision," she said. "I must tell Victorio about the horse soldiers. He decides to attack or not."

"Don't tell him. Say that you could not pick up the trail."

"You want me to lie?"

"Yes."

"To my brother?"

"Yes."

"My brother who is an Apache leader?"

"Yes."

"Apache do not lie."

"Not ever?"

"Never."

She explained that it was a matter of personal honor. Truth, for the Apache, was one of their highest values.

I rose and started walking away from Lozen.

"Where are you going?"

"To the soldiers, to warn them."

I heard the click of her pistol as she cocked the hammer. I looked over my shoulder. She had the Colt Dragoon pointed at my head. Our eyes clashed.

"Don't," she said.

"You keep pointing that gun at me, Lozen. Are you really going to shoot me? After we saved the boy?"

A fresh wind blew up from the northwest, and clouds scudded across the sky. A massive storm was brewing, and the air crackled with its aura.

Compassion reshaped Lozen's expression; her eyes seemed to lighten. She eased back the hammer and holstered the pistol.

"Rain," she said. She looked up at the sky, took her blanket from around her waist and draped it over her shoulders.

◙ ◙ ◙

We found shelter under a stone shelf just as the sky opened and the rain was unleashed. We sat a few feet apart, wrapped in our individual blankets. Sleep was impossible because of the cold and the wind; rivulets of water ran down my back.

"He is to be my husband," Lozen said.

"Who?"

"The sick boy."

"Mazel tov."

"What?"

I explained that it was a Hebrew blessing.

Lozen thanked me, but her voice betrayed no sign of joy.

"You don't sound very happy," I said.

She shook her head and said, "I do not want him. Victorio has chosen him for me. He says that the boy will be a great warrior someday."

"Can't you say no?"

"Yes, I can. All Apache women have the right to refuse a marriage, but…" Her voice trailed off.

"But you want to honor your brother," I filled in for her.

"How did you know?"

"Because that's exactly how it is with the Jews," I said.

In the darkness, her eyes shone as if lit by some internal light.

"Geronimo is a fine young brave," said Lozen, "but I will never love him. He is more like a brother."

"So love is important for the Apache?"

Lozen chuckled. "Is love important for Jews?"

"Of course."

"So why would it not be important for Apache?"

"How does an Apache recognize love?" I asked.

"It is a feeling, it is a touch, and it is when two people no longer have to speak to understand each other."

I looked at her and nodded. Something dark and warm moved in my chest, a teasing phantom. I had never felt anything like this before. My head suddenly felt light, as if filled with white rolling fog. Lozen touched my hand.

"Your hand is cold," she said.

I could only nod.

Her skin was like a furnace, and I immediately pulled away from her.

"What's wrong?" she asked.

"This isn't right."

"What?"

"Touching you. It's... it's..."

"Forbidden?"

"Yes."

"By the laws of your people?"

"Yes."

"It is forbidden by Apache law too."

"So why did you do it?"

"It is how I am, Ariel. I fight all laws. Not just white laws, but Apache customs. It is how Ussen made me. Victorio says that I am wild like the mountain lion."

"I'm not like you, Lozen. I cannot break the laws of my people. The guilt I feel is too deep."

"Guilt is for old women."

"No, Lozen, guilt is good. It makes us act with kindness."

"The white man has no guilt. He has no kindness. Apache cannot afford to be soft. If we are, we will perish."

We stayed separated by a few feet. But I could almost

feel her heartbeats pounding in rhythm with mine. On and off during the long night we managed to snatch a few precious minutes of sleep. When Lozen slept her breath came slow and sibilant, like a gentle wind from the sea.

In the morning, the sky was clear and the air had a fresh scent, like a mountain stream. In silence, we rode back to the Apache camp. We said nothing about our night together under the granite shelf. It was as if we had both risen from a dream and its details were forgotten. But something had happened between us; something in the universe was different, and neither Lozen nor I had any idea how to define this change. We had no idea what it meant; we only knew that we were forever changed.

◙ ◙ ◙

Back in the camp, Mama and Papa greeted me with hugs and then angry words. Why didn't we return? What happened to us? They were sure that we had been murdered. What did Lozen and I do out there in the desert? And how dare I spend the night with an Apache savage?

"She's not a savage," I said to Mama.

"She's a wild child," said Mama. "Pack up, Victorio says we can go. The boy is healed, good as new. Let's get out of here."

Out of the corner of my eye, I saw Lozen conferring with Victorio. No doubt, she was telling him the exact location of Captain Peterson's troop. She had to. Apache do not lie. Not ever.

As we prepared to leave, Lozen approached me to say goodbye. She held out her hand. In it was her brother's bracelet.

"Victorio wants you to have this," she said.

I examined the lovely turquoise stones, the delicate engraving of animals.

"If you should come across Apache braves, show them this bracelet, and they will spare you."

Lozen fastened the bracelet around my wrist.

"You told him the truth, didn't you?"

She nodded.

My heart sank. Captain Peterson, Private Schulman and all the other soldiers would soon be dead. I felt as if I were partly responsible for the coming slaughter.

"I told Victorio the truth about the rain," said Lozen.

"The rain? I don't understand."

"The rain, it washed away the soldiers' trail. I could not find them."

My heart leaped. Lozen smiled, her eyes twinkled.

"Thank you," I whispered.

"For what?"

"Sparing their lives."

"I did not do it for them, Ariel; I did it for you."

◙ ◙ ◙

Once again, we were on the move, rattling along the narrow trail. In the distance were towering mesas. Eagles nested on red buttes, dust devils danced. I walked beside the wagon.

Toward noon, as the sun burned overhead, we came upon a pole-and-adobe cabin hard by a curve in the river. Whoever lived there was not having an easy time. The cabin tilted hard to the side and seemed to be sinking into the earth. Heat had parched and withered the corn and other vegetables in a cultivated patch. The powdered bones of animals long dead were scattered about. A thin stripe of chimney smoke rose steady and pale from a tin cutout in the adobe roof. A young man stepped out of the cabin. He was holding a double-barreled shotgun. Raising it to his shoulder, he sighted down the barrel and aimed at Papa's heart.

"Reckon you gone far enough, pilgrims. One more step and I'll shoot you where you stand."

Chapter 8
—· A Curious Situation ·—

Papa raised his hands and told the young man that we were unarmed and meant him no harm.

The young man squinted at Papa.

"Keturah, come look here," he said, still keeping the gun trained on us.

A young woman came out of the cabin. She wore a tattered gingham dress and a straw sunbonnet. Her feet were bare and filthy. She was raw, work-hardened, her youthful beauty fast fading.

"Good Lord, Jeremiah," she gasped as her eyes fastened on Papa, "what manner of man is he?"

"Don't rightly know. You a white man?" asked Jeremiah, the man with the gun.

"I am," said Papa, "a Jew."

The young couple exchanged astonished looks. I saw the man's finger tightening on the trigger, and I stepped in front of Papa.

"This is a great and holy rabbi," I proclaimed. "To harm

this man would be a sin which your God would never ever forgive!"

The barefoot girl squinted through the sun. Long and hard she stared at Papa.

"Rabbi? Is that like a preacher man?"

"Much greater than any preacher," I cried. My jaw felt suddenly unhinged. "Rabbi Isaacson is from a great line of rabbis, each and every one of them saintly men; a line that traces its lineage all the way back to King David. He is known far and wide as a man of goodness, a noble man with a direct connection to God and his angels." Papa winced, firing invisible daggers at me.

"Oy vey," muttered Papa under his breath. "What are you doing, Ariel?"

The gun was lowered. The girl inched forward. Squinting, concentrating hard, she examined Papa from head to foot. The intensity of her gaze was unsettling. What was she looking for? What did she expect to find in Papa's slight frame?

"What's a rabbi do?"

"Do?" Papa stroked his beard. "I learn Torah. I perform mitzvahs."

She did not understand, and her voice turned peevish. "Speak plain, sir; do you marry, baptize and bury folks like a proper Christian preacher man?"

"We do not baptize," said Papa, "but I do marry, and I do bury, and I am a very fine mohel."

"Mo-what? What language are you speaking? Or are

you some foreigner, unfamiliar with the simple words of God-fearing country folk?"

"Mohel. It means that I circumcise little babies."

"Good Lord. That ain't Christian!"

"Indeed, it is not." Papa nodded his head in agreement.

Keturah whispered into Jeremiah's ear. He looked at her quizzically. Again, she whispered into his ear, this time more urgently.

"You reckon?" he said.

She nodded. Just once, but with perfect conviction.

Something changed. Keturah and Jeremiah's suspicious attitude toward us seemed to melt away. Suddenly they were gracious and hospitable. It was very strange. But so genuine were they that soon enough we were sharing our food with them and planning to spend the night on their homestead.

Keturah and Jeremiah were settlers from Missouri. They told us that they had been living in the territory for a year and a few months.

"It's a hard life," said Jeremiah.

"Them Apache's what make it so," added Keturah. "That Victorio and his evil sister, Lozen, are the scourge of the territory. They are murderers, spoilers of women and a tool of the devil hisself."

I told them that we'd met Lozen. Keturah's jaw dropped in surprise.

"That ain't possible," said Jeremiah, "or'n you'd be separated from your hair an' kilt."

"Actually," I said, "she was very polite. We had a nice discussion."

"Sha-shtill," said Mama.

Keturah kicked Jeremiah under the table. She tried to do it secretly, but she kicked so hard that Jeremiah yelped. There was a tiny battle of eyes between the young couple. Finally, Jeremiah turned to Papa and politely asked if he could speak to Papa, "real private-like."

They stepped off into the silvery darkness. Keturah busied herself with patching some clothing. Anxiously looking over her shoulder, she was nervous as a bird.

Papa and Jeremiah strolled by the creek. It seemed that Jeremiah was doing all the talking. Papa just nodded his head, stroked his beard. And then Papa abruptly stopped in his tracks. His spine stiffened. I could tell that Papa was taken aback.

◙ ◙ ◙

Papa explained what Jeremiah was saying to him.

"He wants to be a chossen," Papa told me.

I looked at him, astonished.

"Jeremiah?"

"And Keturah wants to be a kallah."

"You mean they're not married?"

Papa nodded. No, they were not married. But Jeremiah and Keturah wanted to be bride and groom.

As Jeremiah explained to Papa, he and Keturah had fled from the hills of Missouri, where families were bitterly split between the blue and the gray, where neighbors murdered and lynched and burned one another with frightening savagery and alarming regularity. Jeremiah's family was for the Union and Keturah's kin were for the Rebel cause. They were prohibited from seeing one another. Both were threatened with death if they so much as spoke. So they ran away together, settling in the American West, in the fierce Arizona Territory. But they had not had the opportunity to get married. Not yet. And living in sin was not an option for these two young people. Jeremiah slept outside at night, and when it rained, he would huddle under a tarp.

"Preachers is few and far between in these here parts," Jeremiah informed Papa.

Papa asked why they didn't just go into Tombstone and find a minister to perform the service. Jeremiah explained that they couldn't afford to leave their farm. Who would milk the cow, feed the chickens, and farm the land? A trip to Tombstone and back would take at least five days. And besides, with Victorio and Lozen on the warpath, traveling was perilous.

So Keturah and Jeremiah had waited and prayed for a traveling minister to come through, but so far, no one had come.

Until Papa.

※

Chapter 9

— The Barefoot Bride —

The following morning, Papa told Jeremiah that according to our law, according to halacha, he and Keturah were already considered as married—as long as they had made a personal commitment to one another.

This did not satisfy Jeremiah. He explained that he and Keturah needed a ceremony, something official. "Or she will not share a marriage bed with me," said Jeremiah in a pained voice. "And I don't mind telling you, but this is right difficult. Keturah's a mighty attractive girl, and I don't know how long I can hold out before I plum bust."

"You won't bust," said Papa. "Though you might get a little meshugah."

"Got to make an honest woman of Keturah," he insisted. Again, Papa told him that since he was Jewish and they were Christian, it would be better for them to find a man of their own faith.

"Looky here, Rabbi Isaacson. We got us a problem. We can't go explorin' the territory for no preacher man. There just ain't none out here. Now I'd really appreciate it if'n you'd dust off your preacher duds and get us hitched."

Under Jeremiah's relentless pressure Papa finally told them he would consider their request.

"I have become rabbi to the goyim," Papa lamented as he hefted a stack of his books and settled on a rock beside the creek. Every once in a while he would look up from the page and study the sun's dancing reflection on the water.

Papa scoured his books. He studied the *Even Ha-ezer*; he plumbed the depths of the *Shulchan Aruch*; he looked to see what Maimonides would have to say on the matter. Papa remained motionless over the worn leather volumes for a long time.

"What's he doing?" asked Larke Ellen.

"Looking for guidance."

"I got guidance for your pa." I followed Larke Ellen's gaze. Jeremiah was nervously pacing beside Keturah who sat in the shade of a cottonwood biting her nails and digging her toes into the sand. "All the guidance your pa needs," continued Larke Ellen, "is in the barrel of that scattergun Jeremiah's totin'. Seems to me unless your pa agrees to do the marrying right quick, there's gonna be a grave to be dug."

Papa rose and waved Jeremiah over.

"One hour after sundown, you will have your ceremony."

Jeremiah's wind-scoured face broke into a sunny smile. He looked over at Keturah and nodded. She broke into great heaving sobs.

As I watched the tears drop from her eyes, I realized that Jeremiah's threat to shoot Papa was just that; an empty threat. He never would have done it. And I suspect that Papa, deep in his heart, knew it too.

◎ ◎ ◎

The bride was barefoot. Rebecca gazed at Keturah's narrow little feet, sighed, and tugged off her own high button shoes. Keturah looked at them in disbelief. "For the ceremony," said Rebecca.

"They're right soft and pretty," Keturah said as she slipped them on her feet.

"Papa is a bootmaker," Rebecca offered. "A very fine shoemaker. Back in Russia there was a waiting list for his boots."

Keturah stared at the shoes on her feet as if gazing at precious diamonds. When she took her first step, she stumbled like a toddler.

Embarrassed, she said, "Ain't real used to 'em." She took Rebecca's hand and squeezed hard. "I'm right thankful."

Rebecca washed Keturah's hair in vinegar and brushed it—a hundred firm strokes—till it shone as if lit from within.

Mama took out her sewing box and fashioned a bridal veil out of bits of lace and linen. Her needle flashed in the dying light. Keturah slipped the veil on as if it were a precious tiara. Larke Ellen offered to be a bridesmaid, but

when she tried to stand up, her legs crumbled, and she was shot through with pain. Mama ordered her to remain in the back of the wagon with her baby. "And give that baby a name already!" Mama scolded.

Jeremiah unsnarled his hair with a comb made of thorns. I held up a piece of dull tin as a mirror.

"How do I look?"

"Very nice."

"I'm surely nervous."

"It is your wedding."

"But ain't we terrible sinners, running away like we did?"

"Maybe, maybe not. On the one hand..."

"You folks, you sure don't hold with a simple yes or no, now do you?"

"Well, that depends, you see..."

He broke into laughter and slapped his thigh. I smiled too.

"So tell me, button, what advice you Jewish folks give to a marrying man like me?"

There was a yearning in his eyes, a helpless pleading. He was as vulnerable as any man or woman I had ever seen.

"Have you heard of the Kabbalah, Jeremiah?"

"Can't say that I have."

"It's the book of mystical Jewish tradition. It was given to Moses at Mount Sinai, whispered into his ear by God at the same time as he was given the Ten Commandments. The Kabbalah spends a great deal of time discussing the male and female aspects of God."

Jeremiah scratched the stubble on his chin.

"Sounds right confusing."

"It is. But there is one part of the Kabbalah that is very simple and very clear. It talks about the holiness of marriage."

Jeremiah looked at me with wide eyes. "Holiness?"

I nodded. "Man and woman together are a holy and mystical union. It is also supposed to be…" I searched for the right word. "Agreeable."

"How old are you, button?"

"Almost bar mitzvah."

He frowned, not comprehending.

"Almost thirteen," I explained. "Anyway, Jeremiah, the Kabbalah instructs the man to be nice, to love his wife, to make her happy."

His eyes clouded with confusion. "Happy, you mean I should tell her some humorous stories?"

"Humor is good. But what the Kabbalah means is that man and woman should become as if one person."

Jeremiah scratched his head.

"That sounds right puzzling. You got any suggestions on how I should go about doin' this oneness?"

"I don't know, Jeremiah. After all, I am only twelve years old."

Jeremiah smiled and heaved an exhausted sigh. He straightened his shoulders. "You Hebrew folk sure have some strange ways. But I reckon the good Lord sent you here to bind Keturah and me together in holy matrimony. And for that I am mighty grateful."

Papa beckoned impatiently.

Jeremiah took my hand and shook it vigorously. "I'm beholden to you, button. You've calmed the soul of a fearful man. Though I do wish you'd have not brought up that affair of makin' her happy. Makes me feel untutored."

"I'm sure you'll figure it out when the time comes, Jeremiah."

Jeremiah thought this over, then buttoned the frayed collar of his boiled wool shirt. "Lead me to my bride," he said.

I walked with Jeremiah to the edge of the river, where Papa was waiting.

◙　◙　◙

Papa chanted in Hebrew and Aramaic; Jeremiah and Keturah looked stunned. As Papa continued, they looked perplexed. When it became clear that Papa had no intention of switching to English, Jeremiah interrupted.

"Now just a minute, we can't savvy one single word you're spoutin'."

Papa stopped in mid-sentence. He thrust his face forward and said with steely calm, "You ask a Jew for a wedding, you get Jewish!"

"But—"

"You want me to stop?"

That's when Keturah spoke up.

"No! Please no! Oh, Jeremiah, I feel just like in the Bible! No Christian woman could ask for more."

Papa flinched.

For a good three or four minutes more, Papa chanted in a lovely singsong. Finally, he stopped and declared in English: "You are married."

Jeremiah shook his head as if waking from a dream. Keturah freely wept.

"You are married," Papa repeated.

Jeremiah leaned over to kiss Keturah, but Papa's hand intersected their lips.

"What the hell?" demanded Jeremiah.

"Modesty," Papa explained.

"Good Lord, Rabbi, we're married!" Jeremiah cried.

"And since when does modesty stop in marriage?"

Keturah bowed her head and exclaimed that the rabbi was right. She was going to be a good and modest woman. She thanked Papa. Keturah walked over to Rebecca and tugged off the borrowed shoes, saying, "Much obliged." Keturah's fragile face looked up at Mama. "Would it be too much to ask for a hug, see'n as how my ma ain't here?"

I held my breath. Mama was not the least sentimental. But she opened her arms wide as the world and crushed Keturah to her ample bosom. "What do I do now?" whispered Keturah in a tiny, frightened voice.

"Fulfill the first commandment in the Bible," said Mama.

Keturah frowned.

"Be fruitful and multiply," Mama said and kissed Keturah wetly on both cheeks. "Mazel tov," whispered Mama. "Mazel tov."

Keturah and Jeremiah walked to their adobe cabin. In the silvery moonlight they floated like ghosts. Tiny figures in a terrible landscape. Timid souls about to bind into one.

◎   ◎   ◎

I woke in the middle of the night to the sound of a baby crying. I checked on Larke Ellen and her baby. They were both fast asleep. The sound of the crying infant rose and carried on the evening breeze. I realized that the sound was coming from somewhere out in the desert. The weeping sent chills up and down my spine. I approached a stand of giant saguaro cactus, where the sound seemed to be coming from.

Abruptly the crying stopped.

Above the cactus there was a high shelf of cliffs. I saw two yellow dots of light gliding in the shadows. The Kabbalah warns of shaydim, ghosts, which lurk in deserted spaces. Was I about to meet a ghost of the American West?

"Hello?" I managed to whisper. The rabbis teach us that it helps to speak softly to shaydim, that restless spirits might not do violence if you express sympathy with them.

There was no answer. In spite of the cold desert night air, I was sweating.

"Is anybody up there?"

My voice was weak and trembled like an autumn leaf in the wind.

A shadow detached itself from the rocks. A high-pitched scream tore through the air. Something large and terrible flew right at me.

Its fangs were bared and dripping; its eyes were large as dinner plates, and a thick coat of golden skin rippled with the thrust of powerful muscles.

All this I saw in less than a heartbeat. And in less than a heartbeat I thought to myself, Ariel, say a prayer, because you are going to die.

"Shema Yisroel, Hashem Elokenu, Hashem Echad..."
"Listen, Israel: the Lord is our God, the Lord is One..."

Chapter 10

—· Lozen Revealed ·—

The monster made a strange sound as it crashed into me. It was almost a sigh. I felt the beast's breath—hot and foul—on my face as I crumpled to the earth beneath its massive bulk. A roar thundered in my ears. The beast twitched convulsively, its paws scrabbled against dirt, its head jerked up for a snarling second, the tail lashed; then suddenly blood surged from its mouth, and the beast lay still.

There was silence.

Trapped beneath the creature's suffocating weight, I stared at the sky, at the millions of winking stars. I was alive, still alive. And then I heard soft footsteps approaching. It was Lozen.

She cut off the beast's tail, kneeled and wiped the bloody knife in the desert sands, then secured the grisly trophy to her deerhide belt.

The Apache maiden bent down to my astonished face.

"Are you hurt?"

I shook my head. "I—I don't think so."

She grabbed me under the shoulders and tugged hard, pulling me free from the animal's dead weight. I tried to get to my feet, but my legs felt like rubber and collapsed beneath me. I looked over at the beast. It was a mountain lion, a single arrow buried deep in its heart.

"I thought it was a baby. A crying baby," I offered.

"The mountain lion was crying for food. You were almost the meal." Lozen smiled. I looked at her with a sort of awed wonder.

"You saved my life." It was with great effort that I kept my voice steady.

Lozen said nothing. The very ground on which she stood seemed to exhale silence.

"What are you doing out here?" I probed.

She gazed at me earnestly.

"I mean, how did you manage to be here, right now?"

"This is my home." Lozen replied. Her arm swept in a wide circle indicating the entire desert. "This, all this is home to Mimbres and Chiricahua Apache."

"Yes, I know, but—have you been following us?"

After a long moment, Lozen nodded, just once.

"Why?"

"Stand up now," she ordered.

With Lozen's help, I was able to struggle to my feet. There was blood, a great deal of sticky wet blood, on her hands.

"Why do you look at me like that?" she asked.

"Like what?"

"With fear." Her voice carried an unmistakable challenge.

I shifted uncomfortably. Lozen gazed placidly at me.

"They say that you and your brother—that you and Victorio—are cruel."

"Do you believe this?"

I did not know what to believe or what to think. Why was she out here in the dark? Was she planning on killing us in our sleep? And if that were so, then why did she bother to save my life?

She broke the silence. "The missionaries tell Apache that your tribe killed their God. That your tribe is evil."

My heart sank. Even here, even deep in Apache territory the old lies, the old hates had managed to follow us.

"Do you believe that?" I asked.

"If your tribe killed Christian God, then you have very great power. Apache admire power," she said reasonably.

Sighing, I shook my head. No, no, this was not right. This was all wrong. "Lozen, we did not kill any god. Besides, how can you kill a god? If you kill a god, then he's not much of a god, is he?" In frustration I added, "We didn't kill anybody, Lozen. We're the ones who are always being killed."

"Then why do missionaries say so?"

"Because they can never forgive us for not accepting their god."

"The missionaries say that the whole world hates your tribe. That no land is home to your people."

Feeling bold, I stepped forward and put my face very close to Lozen's. "Are you cruel, are you savages, are the Apache no better than dogs?"

Lozen stiffened. Her eyes flashed with mounting anger, and I feared that she was going to stab me with her knife. "You see," I continued, "half of what they say is lies—and the other half is not true."

Lozen nodded thoughtfully. I studied her face in the pale moonlight. Her wide mouth and high cheekbones gave her an aspect of highborn nobility. Her mahogany skin was silken smooth. But it was her eyes, always her eyes, black and bottomless, that held me. They were the eyes of a girl who has glimpsed hidden worlds through a clear glass.

"You know what I think?" I said.

She looked at me.

"I think we should trust each other."

"Apache never trust white-eyes," she said.

"I am not a white-eye. I am a Jew."

She pinned me with a long and dark gaze. I felt her eyes going right through me, deep into my soul.

"Trust," said Lozen softly, "is nothing but words carried away on the wind."

Lozen turned to walk away. Her horse was tied to a mesquite bush a few yards back. She hopped up on the horse's back.

"Wait," I shouted and ran over to her.

She looked down at me. "Thank you," I said. "Thank you for saving my life."

Lozen nodded. She gripped the reins and prepared to ride off.

"Lozen?"

She looked at me. I just had to know.

"Why have you been following us?"

She heaved a sigh, hesitated a moment, and then said, "I want power."

"Power?"

She nodded gravely. "You have power."

I looked at her in disbelief.

"You have medicine, you have power. I want to learn to take it. I want to learn how to use it. And you will teach me."

The Apache maiden sawed hard on the reins and galloped off into the night.

Papa was not going to like this. He was not going to like this at all.

I ran back to tell Papa what had happened, but when I came to the wagon a fearful moan reached my ears.

I peered over the rim of the wagon tongue. Larke Ellen was shaking uncontrollably. Her right hand, caught in a fearful spasm, was beating a failing rhythm on the plank floor.

I looked closer.

Larke Ellen's blanket was soaked in blood.

�֎

Chapter 11

— Larke Ellen Makes a Request —

Mama took one look at Larke Ellen and said, "She's hemorrhaging."

A horrifying flow of blood poured from beneath Larke Ellen's body. It was black and slick like oil. Mama took charge, snapping out orders. She told Rebecca to boil water. Keturah and Jeremiah's wedding night was rudely interrupted. Keturah was given the job of ripping up strips of cloth to use as bandages. "Let's carry her into the cabin," suggested Jeremiah. "No," said Mama, "there's no time. I have to try and stop the bleeding now. Better she stay where she is." Papa and Jeremiah stood by helplessly. Mama shot Papa a look.

"Say tehillim, Papa."

Nodding almost gratefully, Papa dug his siddur out of his caftan. He swayed rhythmically and chanted Psalms.

"And me?" Jeremiah asked Mama.

"Just do not get in the way."

Mama turned to me. "Her face, Ariel, wipe her face."

I edged over and pressed wet rags to Larke Ellen's skin. Larke Ellen's eyes lifted and held me in their gaze. Her face was wet with a mixture of tears and perspiration. She whispered something. I moved closer, placed my ear next to her lips.

"G—G—Gabriel…"

"What? What did you say, Larke Ellen?"

"Gabriel. Name him Gabriel."

Larke Ellen's body shuddered as if hit by a wave.

"Mama?" I pleaded. "Do something."

"I can't stop the bleeding," said Mama grimly. "Keturah, more bandages. Hurry." Keturah thrust more strips of thin fabric into Mama's hands. Mama worked furiously tearing away the soaked bandages and replacing them with fresh ones.

Shrugged under the weight of an iron kettle filled with boiled water, Rebecca staggered to the wagon. Alarm etched itself across my sister's face as her eyes took in the world of blood that saturated and dripped through the rough pine planks of the wagon deck.

Larke Ellen fought for breath, her lungs rasped like sandpaper; her gaunt chest rose and fell as she struggled for air.

Cold fingers closed around mine. "Promise me… swear to me…" Larke Ellen gasped.

"What, promise you what?"

"You'll raise my Gabriel as one of yours. You're good people. You gave me charity. Only you. Take my Gabriel. Raise him. I want him to be like you…"

"Like us, what do you mean?"

"A Hebrew."

I stared, dumbfounded.

"You don't know what you're saying, Larke Ellen. You're going to be fine." I sneaked a look at Mama, but her face was haggard and her expression hopeless. She was awash in Larke Ellen's blood. Mama shook her head in despair.

"Ariel, promise me," whispered Larke Ellen urgently.

I looked over at Papa, desperately seeking guidance. He chanted the psalms of David in a strong, clear voice.

"Papa," I cried. "Papa."

He will cover you, and beneath His wings you will be protected; shield and armor is His truth. You shall not be afraid of the terror of the night, nor the arrow that flies by day...

Papa's voice echoed and ricocheted off the surrounding cliffs.

Larke Ellen's skin had turned the color of parchment, almost transparent. Perspiration matted her hair. Each tiny detail of her appearance etched itself in my memory like pages in a picture book. Here was her pale skin; here the light fading from her liquid gray eyes; here, damp ringlets of her cinnamon hair glittering with tiny jewel-like globes; and here her callused hands, caked with blood, clutching my wrist in a steely grip.

"Promise me, Ariel. Promise," Larke Ellen demanded.

I looked at Mama. Helpless, she shook her head. "I'm

sorry, I'm sorry," she murmured. Rebecca shook her head, not knowing what to say. My sister's lovely soft hands flew up to her face. Tears spilled from between her fingers.

Larke Ellen's eyes, wide with terror, locked me in their gaze.

"You're the only folks I can trust," she whispered.

Time seemed to stand still. My heart was thumping. Boom. The blood pounding in my ears. Boom. Boom. And then I could feel the spaces between my heartbeats. Boom. Boom. Boom.

How could this be happening to Larke Ellen? She was only seventeen years old. And why was no one helping me? How could I be expected to make such an awesome decision? I trembled. Larke Ellen pulled my hand up to her face, kissed my fingers. The terrible heat of her lips spread through my body, into my heart, into my soul.

"Please, Ariel, please..." she begged. Tears puckered from my eyes. I blinked and struggled for control. My stomach churned.

"I—I promise."

Larke Ellen managed a limp smile. Her whole body seemed to relax.

"What day of the week is it?" she asked.

I thought for a moment.

"Tuesday, I think it's Tuesday."

Larke Ellen's eyes opened wide with astonishment. She looked puzzled.

"It sure don't look like Tuesday," she said.

Her head slumped to the side as all the strength drained from her in one convulsive moment.

Larke Ellen was dead. I continued to hold her hand, to stroke it. A fly settled on her lips. I swatted it away, but it and many others returned almost immediately.

"*Baruch dayan emet,*" murmured Papa. *Blessed is the True Judge.*

◎ ◎ ◎

The next morning, Papa instructed me to dig a grave. He told Jeremiah to hammer together a marker. "Write her name and the Christian year," said Papa. Jeremiah ran his fingers through his hair. "I can fashion the marker, but I don't have the learning to write the words," he said. Papa looked at Keturah. She shrugged. "Them that know their letters is blessed," she said.

"I'll do the writing," sighed Rebecca.

"And I will purify the body," said Mama.

Digging in the baked earth was hard work, but I was glad for it. It kept my mind off the searing pain that was burned into my heart. And what of the promise I had made to her? What would Papa say? Did I do the right thing? Did I have the right to make such a promise? And would Papa and Mama agree to raise little Gabriel as one of their own? And what of my promise to raise him as a Jew? Was that even permissible?

The sun was blazing mercilessly. Sweat ran down my back and soaked my shirt, gluing it to my skin. I felt lightheaded, dizzy. I could still feel Larke Ellen gripping my wrist, still feel the scalding heat of her lips on my fingers, still experience my heart slamming in my chest as if ready to burst.

I stopped digging and looked around at the vast and terrible American wilderness; a landscape at once bleak and noble, lifting the mind into an awareness of enormous desolation; a landscape of terrible opaque distances; a horizon burnt ochre and drab yellow, with mountains that stood ashen in the acrid air.

It was Wednesday. It did not look like Wednesday.

Papa climbed to the bluff where I was digging the grave. He handed me a canteen, told me to sit and rest, that he would do some of the digging. I protested feebly, but Papa was adamant. He did not want me to get sunstroke.

As Papa heaved earth from the shallow pit, I remembered all the graves that had to be dug after the pogrom. Whole families were buried, one after the other, in long terrible columns, rows that inscribed a fearful geometry on the earth.

I looked down at the shack. Mama had finished bathing Larke Ellen's corpse. And now she was dousing water on herself in the creek. She held baby Gabriel in her arms and playfully sprinkled water on his belly. The baby cooed. Mama smiled. The sound of digging had halted. I turned. Papa too was watching Mama. And in his eyes, oh, what grief.

"You made a promise to Larke Ellen?" he asked.

I nodded.

"An extremely serious promise, yes, Ariel?"

"Yes, Papa."

"The question is: was Larke Ellen clear-headed? Did she know what she was saying, or was she confused?"

"I think she was rational, Papa."

"You cannot just think, Ariel, you must be sure."

What Papa was saying was that he would honor my promise to Larke Ellen only if she was in her right mind when she made her dying request. If Papa felt that she made her plea and did not know what she was saying, he would be duty bound to ignore her entreaty.

"Much as it would pain me," admitted Papa, "we would have to bring Gabriel to an orphanage, a Christian home, and let them take responsibility for the baby."

"Papa, no!"

"It is the halacha."

"Oh, Papa. You would not bring Larke Ellen's baby to strangers. No, that can't be right!"

"You must take your time," Papa said.

Larke Ellen's feverish eyes floated in my mind's eye. She was dying, and she was aware of it. *You're the only folks I can trust*, she said.

Trust.

I opened my mouth to speak, but Papa cut me off.

"Wait until we have buried Larke Ellen," he said earnestly. "It is an awesome responsibility that has befallen you."

"Maybe I am too young," I suggested hopefully. But Papa reminded me that I was almost bar mitzvah, and accordingly soon to be considered as a Jewish man—

accountable for all my actions. No longer would my sins fall on Papa's shoulders. To be a Jewish man is to accept responsibility for one's actions.

Sensing the commotion in my heart and mind, Papa scrambled out of the shallow grave and drew me into a warm embrace. The mingled odors of sweat, dust and desert heat filled my head like some overpowering perfume. His wool shirt made my nose itch.

"Ariel, Ariel," he murmured. "How I wish I could make this easier for you."

"You can, Papa. Tell me what to do," I pleaded.

Sadly, Papa shook his head.

"I cannot."

I looked up and gazed into his fathomless brown eyes. "Besides," he teased good-naturedly, "are you not the fearless Hebrew Kid?" I tried to drag a smile across my lips but failed.

Little Gabriel's future, the future of our family, lay with me and me alone.

I was afraid.

According to halacha, a Jew is obligated to bury a Christian and provide a proper service. The hesped, the eulogy, is especially important. The first patriarch of the Jewish people, Abraham, eulogized his wife Sarah, and that has been the custom of Jews ever since. Following the example of Abraham, the purpose of the eulogy is to praise the departed for his or her good qualities, and to express the grief and sense of loss that the mourners are feeling.

Papa explained that the eulogy must be kara'ui, balanced and appropriate. It may not exaggerate or invent qualities that the deceased did not have. Such praise would be a mockery, said Papa, rather than a tribute. In addition, the mourners should remember that although the deceased may have been lacking certain moral qualities, there is always a substratum of goodness and decency in all men that can be detected if properly sought.

Papa spent all morning preparing Larke Ellen's hesped. He sat in the shade of the wagon and scratched words on a scrap of paper. Then he rose to his feet, paced back and forth, his hands locked behind his back, absorbed in his thoughts. Finally, just as the sun was beginning its slow plunge behind the distant mountains, Papa gestured that it was time.

We gently lowered Larke Ellen's body into the grave. She was wrapped in a water-stained canvas sheet that had been used to cover furniture in our wagon. There was no wood from which to make a coffin. I kept waiting for Larke Ellen to sit up and say, "Now wait a minute, this is a mistake." As if death were a game of hide-and-seek. I looked at her wrapped corpse. Was Larke Ellen really in there? It seemed unreal, like a bad dream. Perhaps if I stared hard enough, perhaps if I hoped hard enough, perhaps by willing it hard enough, she would come back to life. And even as I hoped, even as I felt my heart bursting with grief, I knew that I would never see Larke Ellen again. Never again would I see tiny slivers of sunlight dance through her rust-colored hair. I missed her endless questions, I missed the way she teased me, and I missed the sparkling laugh that slipped from her lips so softly and easily, the song of a bird. We all stood at the edge of the shallow grave, Mama, Rebecca, Jeremiah, Keturah, Papa, and I.

"Her name was Larke Ellen," said Papa. His voice was barely above a whisper. "She came to us and asked for work after her husband passed away. We hired her as a maid, but soon enough it became clear that she had become something else. We who have lost so much in the past few years found ourselves blessed with another family member. Yes, Larke Ellen became a member of our family. To Mama and me, she was like a daughter-in-law. For Rebecca and Ariel, a lively and good-natured sister. Larke Ellen was a good and kind soul. She was not educated, but she was bright, very bright. She asked questions, one after the other, and the sages teach us that he who asks the right questions is more blessed than he who gives the answers.

"Larke Ellen was a good mother. This is very important, her most important quality, because as she lay dying, her only request, her only concern was the welfare of her baby. She did not beg God to spare her life. She did not ask for there to be less pain, she did not even ask God to forgive whatever sins she might have committed. No, all she could think about was the welfare of her child. For this and this alone, I am sure that Larke Ellen has earned her share in the world to come. We will all miss her."

Rebecca dabbed at her eyes with a corner of her apron.

Mama wept into the baby's soft, fuzzy head. Keturah leaned into Jeremiah, and tears slid down her cheeks. Hot tears gushed from my eyes.

Surely happiness and loving-kindness will follow me all the days of my life, and I shall dwell in the house of the Lord for evermore.

As we shoveled dirt over the grave, I felt the future looming before me like a dragon.

I took a deep breath.

"Papa?"

"Yes?"

"She was perfectly coherent."

"Then in the morning we will have a bris," Papa said.

◎　◎　◎

That night, Mama wrote an amulet engraved with the words "Adam and Eve excluding Lilith." Mama tapped Gabriel on the nose three times and recited her formula seven times.

"What's your Ma doin'?" asked Keturah.

"It's a prayer to protect Gabriel from Lilith."

"Who might that be?"

"Lilith is the demon queen of the night. She is the bride of Samael, master of the evil forces of the sitra achra, the other side."

"The other side of what?"

"The other side of this world. It is the world of demons and evil."

"Sounds right fearful. And who might this Lilith be?"

"Lilith was the first wife of Adam."

"I didn't know ol' Adam had two wives. I thought fer sure that there was just Eve. Is this here in the Bible?"

"It is in the Kabbalah."

"How come Christian folk ain't heard of all this?" Keturah inquired suspiciously.

"Keturah, most Jews have not heard of Kabbalah. It is, for the most part, hidden knowledge. Actually, some rabbis say that you may not study Kabbalah until you are over forty years old. And others say that you must never study Kabbalah. Ever."

"Why not?"

"Because it can make you insane."

Keturah laughed and asked me to tell her more about Lilith.

"Well, Lilith demanded equality with her husband, and when she found she could not get it, she pronounced the hidden name of God and flew away. Adam complained to God, who sent three angels to bring her back. But Lilith refused. Ever since then she flies like a night owl to attack those who sleep alone, to steal children and to kill newborn infants, especially boys who are about to have a bris."

"A what?"

"Circumcision. It is our covenant with God."

"Is that where you cut the pizzle?"

"I guess that is one way of putting it," Papa coolly confirmed.

◎ ◎ ◎

Gabriel cried very little as Papa performed the circumcision. Back in Russia Papa did the bris milah on a regular basis, for he was the village mohel. He used to practice on leather so that the children he circumcised would experience as little pain as possible.

Gabriel was now a Jew. Gabriel had eyes as gray as Larke Ellen's, eyes the color of rain clouds, and soft red curls. Gabriel was tiny, maybe too small, but he had a beautiful round face.

Now I was an older brother.

After the bris, as Gabriel slept, Mama stared at his little face and spit "Tfu. Tfu. Tfu!" and exclaimed in Yiddish, "How ugly!" This was the custom—to insult the baby so as to ward off the evil eye.

At first, when Rebecca held Gabriel, she was stiff, ill at ease, but now Rebecca relaxed, and when she fed the baby a bottle of milk, her eyes never left the baby's face. My sister, for the first time in a long time, seemed content.

"I'm a tante," she said proudly.

"Ariel, say hello to your baby brother," Papa said.

I touched Gabriel's little hand. It opened like a flower; then he held my finger in a tight grip. His eyelids opened, and his deep gray eyes, flecked with gold, took me in. Gabriel smiled and made a gargling noise in the back of his throat. For the briefest of moments I saw Larke Ellen's face hovering over the tiny features of the baby. It was as if

Larke Ellen was looking right at me, beaming behind those lively freckles.

"You're the only folks I can trust."

Those eyes trusted me, trusted all of us. Larke Ellen lived on in little Gabriel.

Chapter 12

—· Tracks ·—

Unable to sleep, I tossed and turned all night long. Finally I crawled out of my blanket, grabbed a volume of the Talmud, and trudged up the slope to Larke Ellen's fresh grave. Below me, the river ran gentle across its stones. The water caught the moon in a rippling blue-gray reflection. Closing my eyes, I inserted my index finger between the thick and silky pages and started to open the Talmud at random.

Footsteps scrabbled behind me, and I turned to see Rebecca climbing the hillside. Her dark woolen shawl fluttered in the wind.

"Are you all right?" she asked.

I nodded.

"But you cannot sleep."

I shrugged.

"Neither can I," she said. "Ariel, what's he doing?"

"Who?"

"Papa, of course."

"I don't understand, what do you mean?"

"Do not play games with me, little brother. Papa tells you things. He confides in you. I want to know what he plans for us, for this family."

I said nothing. I knew that if I told Rebecca about Papa's search for the Lamed Vovniks, she would howl in fury.

"It's not fair, Ariel, letting Papa drag us all across this parched wasteland on some kabbalistic whim."

"It's not a whim."

She seized my wrist. "Aha! So there is some crazy mystical answer to all this. Tell me. Tell me!"

I shook my head from side to side, refusing to answer. And suddenly Rebecca slapped my face. I heard the sharp crack of her palm against my cheek; there was a spiky burst of light behind my eyelids, like a flash of lightning. I barely felt the sting; mostly I experienced a hot flush traveling through my cheeks and down my neck. How is it, I wondered, that my sister's soft, smooth hand was able to strike such a hard blow? My vision blurred, and I realized that tears were pouring out of my eyes. Rebecca was looking at the hand she used to slap me. She was frozen, dazed by what she had done. Then Rebecca folded me in her arms and held me tight.

"I am sorry," she breathed over and over again. "Oh, I am so very sorry."

I don't know how long we stayed like that. Time seemed to stop. All I could hear was the beating of Rebecca's heart and her breath whispering like a song.

"Don't you understand?" she whispered, breaking my reverie. I looked up into my sister's face. It had never occurred to me before, but she was beautiful, with an oval face, full lips, and wide-open eyes, sparkling, perpetually astonished. She seemed to hover over me like an angel.

"Understand what, Rebecca?"

"Papa," she said gently. "He's not well."

"Not well. What do you mean?"

"Papa, he's not right in the head, and if we continue like this, we will all be destroyed."

My heart turned, and I felt my sister's burning lips press against my forehead. I could not remember the last time she had kissed me.

"You're wrong about Papa," I challenged, my voice ragged with tension. "You don't know what you are talking about."

Rebecca held my face in her hand and looked me straight in the eye. "Am I? Am I wrong?"

"Yes, you are. You just don't understand Papa. No one understands him. He's a great man, a great scholar. Papa can—Papa can look down at the sky."

"Perhaps it is time for Papa to look down at the earth."

And with that, Rebecca started walking back to the wagon. My sister halted in her tracks and looked over her shoulder at me.

"What about your bar mitzvah, Ariel? What does Papa plan to do, have it out here in the middle of nowhere? What will you do for a minyan, maybe some Apache Indians? How does that make you feel?"

I had no answer. I had not stopped thinking about my bar mitzvah, to be a Jewish man, to be counted in a minyan, to be responsible for all my actions – oh, how I yearned for that. Moreover, I had waited for Papa to say something, waited for Papa to find a town where we could gather the ten Jewish men who would make a minyan. But Papa had said nothing. And when I would bring up the subject, when I would press Papa for an answer, for a decision, Papa would simply tell me to study my haftorah and to meditate on its meaning.

All was silent as Rebecca skidded down the hillside. I sank to the ground. The feeling of limitless space surrounded me. It was immensity both grand and noble, but all I could think about was finding a snug place to crawl into, a space both warm and safe. Back in Russia when the nights were like ice, when the wind howled demonically and stung like razor blades, I used to climb to a shelf just above the wood stove and curl up into a ball. There was a window right by this shelf, and I would press my face to the icy window and feel my skin tingle and then turn numb. The snow would pile against the glass, and lovely patterns would inscribe themselves against the windowpane. A long, dark tree branch—heavy with snow, brittle with ice—tapped against the roof all night long. It was there on that warm shelf, in dim streaks of moonlight, that I first started to play my Talmud game. It was there that I opened the Talmud at random, curious to see what I would find. It was a game of chance that I played, to see if the page I turned to could have some direct bearing on what I was thinking or doing at that very moment.

Here in the vast Arizona landscape, I indulged in my old diversion.

I opened the Talmud. I closed my eyes, raised my finger and then brought it down, blindly stabbing the page. "What are those tracks?"

I practically jumped out of my skin and whirled around in surprise. There stood Lozen just a few feet behind me. Moonlight glinted off the steel barrel of the rifle that rested in the crook of her arm.

"I didn't hear you."

"You are not Apache." She smiled, then came forward and sat down beside me. She took the Talmud from my hand, opened it. Her eyes scanned the pages. She frowned.

"These tracks, what do they mean?"

"Tracks? Oh, you mean the words, the writing."

"Word-tracks," Lozen said. "What do they say?"

How to explain? I took a deep breath: "This book is one of many called Talmud."

"Tal-mud," she repeated. "What does this word mean?"

"Talmud means study. The Talmud is a record of my tribe's laws and customs, stories and history."

"It is like the white man's law?"

"Ours is much older, and ours was given to us by God."

"God speaks to your tribe?"

"Yes, God speaks to my tribe. Once, he spoke to us through the lips of holy men and women, prophets; now through our holy books."

Lozen ran a finger over the page. "There is power in these words?"

I nodded. "There is a great deal of power in these words. If not for these words, my tribe would be lost."

Lozen gave me a questioning look. I tried to explain:

"My tribe, the Jews, was sent into exile from our tribal lands many years ago. We lived as strangers in strange lands."

Lozen leaned forward and hung on my every word. What I was saying was of immediate interest to the Apache maiden.

"The elders of our tribe realized that unless our laws were written down, there was the danger that the ways of our people would be forgotten. They understood that for a small tribe to survive among larger and more powerful tribes, the Jews had to build a fence—an invisible fence—around the tribe. This fence was made of words and ideas."

Weighing my words, a deep frown creased Lozen's forehead.

"Your fence, is this to keep your tribe in, or to keep the other tribes out?"

I grinned. "Both," I offered. "The fence serves both purposes."

"You have read this Tal-mud, Ariel?"

Chuckling, I leafed through the pages. "You don't read the Talmud, Lozen. You have to *learn* it."

"Are they not the same?"

"Not at all. You can't read the Talmud like a story. You have to study it. You have to use your brain and your heart."

"Ariel has learned it all?"

"No. No one has learned it all."

"Not even the old one?"

"Not even my father. You see, Lozen, the Talmud is a world. It is a world within worlds. Its words are like the stars in the sky, beautiful and endless. Not even the holiest of Jews can know everything in the Talmud. There is always something that is hidden; always there is something which is just beyond our understanding."

Lozen gazed fixedly at the page of Talmud.

"We do not have tracks."

It took me a moment to understand what she was telling me. I found it hard to believe. "You mean the Apache people do not have a written language?"

Lozen nodded. "Our words are free. Our words fly as if on the wings of eagles," she said.

"But Lozen, if you don't have books, if you don't have writing…" My voice trailed off. Sadness filled my heart.

"What?"

I shook my head, not wanting to finish the thought. But Lozen was not one to let anything go without a struggle.

"Say what you were thinking."

"It is not important."

"Then you can say it," she insisted.

"Lozen," I offered, "if we did not have words, and if we had not written our words in books, we would have disappeared off the face of the earth a long time ago."

Her expression did not change. A sudden wind blew in

from the north and lifted Lozen's hair so that it trailed in the wind, delicate black tendrils, like wisps of silk.

The Apache maiden placed the barrel of her rifle across the page of Talmud.

"Maybe Ariel's tribe did not have enough guns to fight their enemies."

I shook my head from side to side.

"Our laws, our customs, our *learning* is stronger than any gun. Swifter than any horse, sharper than any knife."

Not in agreement, but as a way of letting me know that she heard what I was saying, Lozen nodded her head. And at that moment Lozen appeared to me as alone and as isolated as any person I had ever seen. It was as if what I had said abruptly stripped her of the armor which all her life she counted on for protection. It was as if my words were bullets that threatened to puncture not only her flesh, but her very soul. Immediately I regretted everything that I had said to her.

She struggled to clarify her thoughts. "What Ariel is saying is that without tracks on paper, without these words, the Apache will be destroyed?" Her eyes searched mine. I shrugged, unwilling or perhaps unable, to face her conclusion.

"Tell me, Ariel, is that what you see? Will the Apache end up as dust under the heel of the white-eyes?"

"I am not a prophet, Lozen. I cannot say. All I know for certain is that my tribe, the Jews, have managed to survive the most terrible wars and persecutions through the power of our holy words."

The silence was long and heavy. Somewhere in the distance a wolf howled. I fidgeted, uncomfortable. Lozen's eyes were still fixed on the page of Talmud. It was as if she was waiting for the letters to spring to life, to expand off the page and become living breathing things which would take Lozen by the hand and lead her to victory over her enemies.

I reached out with my index finger and scratched shallow moats in the ground.

"What is that?"

"Your name, Lozen, in Hebrew, the language of my people."

She placed the index finger of her right hand in the lamed, the first letter of her name.

"Teach me," she said.

It did not take very long for Lozen to be able to write her own name in Hebrew. As I said, she was smart, and she thirsted for knowledge—any knowledge. For the next hour I showed Lozen the whole Hebrew alphabet. I offered to show her English too, but her expression tightened, her eyes flashed in anger, and she declined to learn the language of the people she hated. The language of the people who were her blood enemies was unclean, she maintained. Besides, what Lozen wanted was power, and Hebrew, the language of the Jews, the language of a tribe that, as I had told her, had suffered and, yes, even flourished through terrible oppressions, was clearly a language endowed with magical and holy powers. And I could not disagree. After all, the Sages teach us that God created the world with the letters of the Hebrew alphabet, words that were written with black flames on white sheets of fire.

◎　◎　◎

Over the next few days, Lozen and I met behind the hill every night and continued her studies.

"Eat this," said Lozen, offering me a dark chunk of meat. Shaking my head, I declined.

"Mule," she said, cutting off a slice with her knife and tipping the meat into her mouth. "Apache like mule much better than white eyes' cattle."

Kosher and non-kosher animals did not seem to perplex Lozen at all. She told me that the Apache also had food they would not eat, even if they were starving to death: snake was considered evil; all fish were regarded as somehow not real food.

The one thing that Lozen found incomprehensible was the commandment against stealing.

"What about stealing horses?" Lozen prodded.

"Stealing anything is wrong," I countered.

Smiling, Lozen proudly told me that horse-stealing was a way of life with the Apache tribes. "And I, Lozen, am one of the best horse thieves of the Mimbres Apache."

"I'm sure you are a wonderful horse thief, Lozen, but it's wrong to take something that belongs to another person."

"White-eyes try to take the land of the Apache."

I took a deep breath. "The white man is wrong. Maybe you should make the white man pay for the land."

Lozen tapped me on the forehead.

"What are you doing?" I cried.

"Looking to see if it is wood."

"What?"

"How can anyone own the earth? Only Ussen owns the land."

"Let's look at it differently," I said, reaching out and prying the knife from her work-toughened fingers. "How would you feel if I stole this knife from you?"

"Bad."

"Right, so stealing is wrong."

"I feel bad because Lozen is not strong enough to stop you from stealing it."

"Lozen, don't you believe in right and wrong?"

"Yes, many rights and many wrongs, but horse-stealing, it is good. It is how we live; it is how we have always lived. Without horse-stealing, the Apache are weak, like silly old women."

Sighing, I shook my head. Nothing I could say or do could bridge the gulf that separated me from the Apache maiden.

"You are angry, Ariel?"

"No."

"Your eyes, they look angry."

"Lozen, would you steal my horse?"

"No."

"Why not?"

"It is a bad horse. It is not worthy of an Apache brave."

"You mean you'd steal a horse that belonged to me if it was a good horse?" I cried.

That's when Lozen's face broke into a huge smile. She was teasing me. And I flushed with embarrassment.

"Lozen would never steal from a friend," she said gently. "To steal from a friend, that would be wrong."

"Is that what we are, Lozen, friends?"

With a direct gaze, she looked at me in silence. Finally she said in a low voice, almost a whisper, "Yes, Ariel. We are friends."

Looking into her face I saw the moon reflected silver and gray in the blackness of her eyes. It gave her the semblance of a ghost.

A cold wind blew from the northern mountains, and I shivered.

※

Chapter 13

—· Keturah Confesses ·—

For several days, Lozen did not appear on the bluff. I missed her, missed our easy conversation, her penetrating questions. Maybe she had lost interest in our friendship. Or perhaps she was with her brother Victorio on a horse-stealing raid across the Rio Grande.

And now, it was Shabbos.

It had just turned dark. White as cream, the moon hung low in the sky. A fine mist lay over the desert.

Right before sundown, Papa and I had greeted the Sabbath queen while praying on the hill right above Jeremiah and Keturah's homestead. When the sun fell, it turned the canyons purple and the junipers gold. After dark, I sat by the wagon, studying my bar mitzvah portion. I shifted uncomfortably; my spine felt pleated by the wagon spokes.

A horse nickered, bobbed its great noble head and snorted milky vapor. Huge gray moths rustled around the single lantern on the side of our wagon. It threw a guttering light. I looked up at the stars, and the sight stirred the slow tide of memory to Russia, to our poor shtetl, our previous land of exile. How far we had come. And yet once again here we are, strangers in another's land. Yet whose land was it? Did it belong to the Apache as Lozen vowed, or did it now belong to the Christian Americans? Eternal questions that seemed to have no fixed answer.

Keturah interrupted my reverie. "What's this you call it—this night, I mean?"

I twisted around to look past the wheel rim.

"Shabbos."

"That's what you call the Sabbath."

"The Sabbath is what you call Shabbos," I assured her.

"You know I never met no Jews before. You're right good folks, which ain't what we was expectin'."

I did not bother asking what Keturah was expecting; I knew all too well. Keturah leaned over and gazed at the page of Hebrew verse I was studying. She frowned.

"What manner of language is that?"

"Hebrew."

"You can savvy that?"

"Yes, I can."

"I got learning up to, oh, third grade, but that's all my folks felt was becoming for a female person. My pa says book learning makes a body arrogant and prideful."

"Book learning is like air, Keturah. Without it you cannot breathe."

Intrigued by what I said she inclined her head and said,

"Teach me something. But something that's right simple. I ain't all that quick. Least that's what my pa opinioned." Her shoulders were bunched up and her eyes watchful like a shy colt.

Thinking for a moment, I asked her, "Do you know where your name comes from?"

"The Bible, I reckon."

"That's right. Keturah was Abraham's second wife. In fact, the rabbis teach us that Keturah was actually another name for Hagar, Sarah's handmaiden. People often had two names in those days. After Sarah died, Abraham married Keturah. She bore him sons, and do you know what they did?"

"Something wicked, I wager. Didn't all those folks commit all manner of sinful abominations?"

"No, not at all. After they were grown up, Keturah's sons, Abraham sent them east. According to our rabbis, the sons of Keturah journeyed east, and there they established all the great religions of that part of the world."

"You mean they got some kind of religion back in New York?"

"East means Asia. China. The land of Japan. India."

Her eyes, sharp and watchful, widened in amazement. "Them is heathens in those far-off lands. What religions they got there? Something other than Christian, I expect."

"Oh, there are many religions in the east. There are the followers of Buddha. There are Hindus. Zoroastrians.

Dozens and dozens of sects that all possess valuable wisdom."

"I never heard such a thing," she said. "You sure you're not having a yarn on me?"

"I promise."

"Well then, your word, that's good enough. I can tell you would not lie. No, sir, you surely would not." She hesitated, narrowed her eyes. "Would you lie to me?"

"No, never."

Smiling, Keturah touched her belly.

"Are you all right?" I asked.

"Just hoping that I will have a son real soon."

"Does it have to be a son?"

"It's what Jeremiah would like. And I'm taking measures to assure him of this."

"What kinds of measures?"

Massaging her belly with the palm of her callused hand, Keturah said, "Granny woman back home told me that it's a boy if'n you conceive on a night of a full moon. So you can believe me, I keep an eye on the night and the stars and the transit of the moon." She lowered her eyes. "I ought not be speakin' like this to you, I know that, and I'm awful sorry. It's hard out here, alone with Jeremiah; he don't talk all that much, and he don't like for me to talk about things which I feel in my heart; it makes him powerful uncomfortable."

"Our sages say that men like to examine and women like to feel."

Keturah brightened. "That's real smart. That's just how it is. I mean, exactly. Take Jeremiah, for instance; he'll fix on a problem for hours, for days, for weeks even, and I can tell it's eating him up inside. I tell him to talk it out with me. I'm your wife—well, *now* I am, thanks to the rabbi — I'm your wife, I say, talk it over with me. You would think that would make sense, common sense. But no, Jeremiah just gets all manner of quiet, stubborn quiet, I call it, and keeps whatever he's feelin' all bottled up inside. Men are like that, I reckon."

"Yes, they are," I said.

"Jewish men too?"

"For that you'll have to ask Mama."

Keturah grinned. She had a truly engaging grin; you couldn't help responding in kind.

"Are you folks heading west?" Keturah asked.

Deciding not to tell her about Papa's dreams, about our search for the thirty-six righteous men, I told her that we had not made up our minds.

"I only ask because you ain't no match for them Apache. You may think that Victorio and Lozen won't lift your scalps, but take it from me, them heathen ain't got feelings like you and me. You turn your back, and chances are good them Apache will slip a knife betwixt your ribs. And there ain't no words to describe what they do to white women. The outrages are most awful. Look here, see this."

Out of her ragged homespun apron, Keturah withdrew a .41-caliber Derringer. "I keep this with me day and night, because if ever I should fall into them savage hands, I would first put a bullet in my brain pan. Tell me, you Jewish folks, what notions you have on killing yourself?"

"I hope it never comes to that, Keturah."

"I take it you don't hold with the idea."

"The rabbis teach us that there are three instances where a Jew must allow himself to be killed. The first is to avoid becoming a worshipper of idols. The second is that you must never kill an innocent person in order to save yourself. The third is that one must first die rather than commit adultery or incest."

"So you would tell me not to put this here Derringer to my head if'n I was stoled by Apache."

"We would tell you to live, to try and escape. But to kill oneself—I don't think so."

"Well, right there I'm glad I ain't a Hebrew. No Apache buck is a-gonna outrage my breathing body. I must admit, puzzlin' on such makes me dreadful sad."

"To contemplate truth without sorrow is the greatest gift," I quoted.

"What's that?"

"If you are able to think about how hard life is without becoming sad, well, it's something of a blessing," I explained.

She lifted her eyes and looked at me. Silvery bars of moonlight were reflected in her eyes. "Who said that?"

"Jewish mystics."

"What's that?"

"Men who try to understand the secrets of the universe."

"I don't know if that's at all possible, leastways not here, not in the Arizona Territory."

I smiled. "No, maybe not."

Twisting a ribbon of black hair like a silken tassel, Keturah shifted uncomfortably. Her eyes darted from my face and then to her lap. "I ain't been entirely truthful," she said in a tiny whisper.

Looking at her I waited for more. Even in the gloom of the night, I could see her face was flushed with embarrassment.

"We lied to you."

"Lied, lied about what?"

"We ain't been entirely pure. As a man and a woman, I mean."

"Keturah, you really don't have to tell me anything more. It's none of my business. And besides, you're married now, it's all in the past."

"No, I want to tell you. Truth is we…"

"Keturah," I pleaded, "please don't."

"Me and Jeremiah," she said, "we kissed a whole lot."

"I see."

"Every night for six minutes. I counted off the seconds in my head so's we didn't go any longer."

"That's all?"

"Not really."

"I don't want to know."

"We held hands and took little walks down by the

stream. Sometimes we kissed and held hands. I reckon we're just sinners. I suppose you're gonna have to go and tell the rabbi what me and Jeremiah done, right?"

"Keturah, you're a fine woman, a fine wife, and someday you will be a wonderful mother. And no, no, I'm not going to tell Papa anything."

She smiled hugely as she acknowledged the compliment. Her eyes flashed, twinkled like snowflakes, and a small cry of joy burst from her lips. It was like the chirp of a bird suddenly set free. Lunging forward, she tried to wrap her arms around me, but I jumped away.

"What's the matter, you afraid of girls?"

"Yes. No. Actually, what I mean to say is that I'm not allowed to touch a woman. Not until I'm married."

"It's not proper," she repeated. "I understand. I surely do." Keturah continued, "I deeply thank you." She smelled of dust and sun, the fragrance of Arizona, of the American West. "Some day," she breathed, "you are gonna make some lucky girl a fine husband."

◙　◙　◙

It was a cool high-desert night. Everyone was asleep but me. The wind blew off the crests of the mountains, scattering some tumbleweed against the side of the wagon, while others nestled into dry basins and parched sinks. Coyotes howled in a draw behind the adobe sod. After Keturah left, I must have fallen asleep under the wagon. Something woke me. A shadow moved on the hill. It was like a giant black butterfly shifting speedily across the moonlit earth.

Screwing up what little courage I possessed, I decided to go and investigate.

Quiet as a leaf, I made my way up the hill.

As I crested the rise, the cold steel of a knife blade was pressed against my throat, and my breath became a frightened sob.

A voice hissed in my ear. "You got food, boy?"

When I tried to speak my voice collapsed into a feeble croak. My answer was neither a yes nor a no, just a pathetic whimper. Finally, whoever was holding the knife to my throat eased back on the pressure.

"You got grub?" a deep male voice growled.

"Yes."

"You go down and bring me some, boy. You don't tell anyone I'm here, because if you do, I'll kill you and your whole family. You got me, boy?"

"Yes, sir."

"You ain't gonna get smart on me, are you, boy?"

"No, sir."

"Y'better not, 'cause I'm the meanest son of a gun in the territory."

I nodded my head.

"Speak up, boy."

"Yes, sir. I understand, sir."

"I'm gonna let go now, and I want you to scoot on down to camp and steal me some meat, bread, and hot coffee."

"Would you like some kugel, sir? My mother makes a delicious potato kugel."

"What is a ku-gall, boy, you tryin' to back-talk me?"

"Oh, no, sir, just recommending my mother's kugel. It's finely grated potatoes, baked into a crispy pie."

"Sounds right fine. Bring me a heap."

The knife fell away from my throat. Strong hands whirled me around. I found myself looking into pale blue eyes, razor eyes the color of polar ice floes. In contrast to his crude and violent speech, my captor was elegant in dress. He wore a blue woolen cape over an ornate silk waistcoat; the striped pants of a dandy fell over expensive hand-tooled Texas boots. His Stetson hat, the color of limestone, was set at a rakish angle on his head. In his hand, the wicked Bowie knife glittered like liquid moonlight. He was thin as a buggy whip, with a long sharp nose, a gaunt beak that made him look like a vulture. Under the canopy of stars, a dark celestial meadow, he had the look of a man possessed.

"Any guns down there, boy?"

"No, sir," I lied, hoping that he would not detect the slight tremor that always shook my voice when I stretched the truth.

He squinted at me, suspicious.

"You wouldn't be fixin' to come on back with some sort of posse, would you, boy?"

"No, sir, absolutely not." I hastened to add, "There's just a farmer and his wife and my family. We are peaceful people."

"If I see iron I'll send you to your judgment. Why you look and talk so funny?"

"I'm from Russia."

"Russia, huh?"

"Yes."

"My word, but you talk peculiar. Now git, and bring them vittles real fast. I got a solid gold watch here in my vest pocket what keeps perfect time. You got three minutes to come on back with my food. One second past three minutes, and I'll come charging into that sodbuster's farm, my two Colts blazing. What do you say to that?"

"I hope your clock doesn't run fast."

As I ran back to the farm, my heart was slamming in my chest, back and forth, back and forth, like an iron fist. A real live outlaw, a desperado, was threatening my life and the lives of my family and my friends. It was both frightening and thrilling. I felt my blood beating. What could I do to thwart this depraved man? What would Lozen, my brave Apache maiden, do if she were caught in the same circumstances?

Chapter 14

—·· Doc ·—

The stranger wolfed down Mama's food. He grunted, sighed with pleasure at the taste of the potato kugel and cholent. He was careful not to splash any on his fine linen shirt.

"Good?"

"Your Ma's a powerful fine cook."

"Thank you. What is your name, sir?"

"Why do you inquire?"

"So we can be friends."

He looked surprised, sat up straight and carefully flicked crumbs from his handlebar mustache.

"Friends? Even though I have scared you, stolen food from you?"

"Sir," I said, "Abraham always fed the hungry who journeyed in the desert. Can I do any less?"

"Abraham who?"

"The biblical patriarch Abraham."

"Oh, that Abraham. My word. I used to read the Bible,

back home with Martha Ann." His voice trailed off and he blinked back—wait, was that a tear that puckered in his eye?

"Good gracious, please forgive my bad manners; my name is John Henry Holliday. They call me Doc."

"Pleased to meet you, Doctor Holliday."

"Just Doc. I was a dentist, trained in Baltimore, but poker is more profitable. Truthfully, I am a formidable sinner, chained to my numerous vices. Allow me to thank you for your kindness."

Lilting and soft, his voice carried the distinctive accent of the Southern states—a gentle wash of elegant tones.

"You are talking differently than before."

"I was trying to scare you, so I used the language of a low-born scalawag."

"Would you like more food?"

Doc Holliday smiled; his smile was the saddest I had ever seen. "No, no, I have feasted quite enough. Many, many thanks, young man. I owe you an explanation. Kindly understand this is most unusual for me. I am not a vagrant, nor a drifter, but a professional gambler—and, to be absolutely truthful, a rather deadly pistoleer."

"What happened, how did you end up alone, without a horse in the middle of nowhere?"

"Big Nose Kate happened."

I did not understand, and I said so. Doc reached into his silken vest, took out a chamois pouch and rolled himself a cigarette.

"Kate Elder. She is my partner and my ruination. Big Nose Kate will be the death of me."

"How big is her nose?"

"Oh, not that big, not really. It is actually quite lovely; a Roman nose, proud and noble, with a charming spray of freckles right across the bridge."

"Then why do you call her Big Nose?"

"A mystery. Truly. That's what she's called and so, lacking imagination, that is how I refer to her."

Doc Holliday looked my way and shook his head as if trying to clear it. "Kate and I left—no, we fled—Dodge City several days ago. The reason? There was a rather unfortunate incident involving five-card stud, a low-down Yankee cheater, my Colt Peacemaker, and, well, Kate's honor."

"You killed a man for cheating at cards after he insulted your wife," I surmised.

Doc chuckled and blew a stream of smoke into the air. "I like you, I most certainly do. You are correct, except for one minor detail: Kate is not my wife. And therein lies the tale. You see, Kate has a brain in her head, and is therefore someone I can talk to about the arts and literature. Her Greek and Latin are quite passable. However, like all women, she wants just one thing: to get married. And from Dodge, on our way to Tombstone, she started in on me. How many times have I told her that I am not the marrying kind? How many times have I told her that if she truly has her sights fixed on marriage, then she should move on, find a nice bank teller, a forgiving preacher, a peaceful merchant.

However, Kate is a stubborn woman. She insists that she will marry me. She comes, I might add, from a royal Hungarian family, and there is a streak of mule in her a mile wide. Well, there we were, riding in the buckboard, mile after dusty mile, and Kate just kept talking and demanding. And I kept drinking my whiskey. Have I mentioned liquor in my narrative? No? Well, the demon rum and I are on intimate terms. Most intimate terms. I can honestly say that between cards, liquor, and the occasional killing, I am perhaps the most debased man you are likely ever to meet.

"To resume: after the liquor was gone, and with Kate babbling endlessly about the joys of marriage, the comforts of hearth and home, I had had quite enough. I told Kate that if she did not cease immediately I would get out of the buckboard. Kate, I should add, is a superb gambler, and so she called my bluff, told me that she did not intend to give up. That, in fact, when we arrived in Tombstone, the first thing she intended to find was not a saloon, as is our usual custom, but a preacher, to marry us. 'Are you ready to get out?' she dared me. 'I am,' I exclaimed. 'Do you know where we are?' she challenged. 'In the dark,' said I. Kate smiled. It is a very seductive smile, and it has broken many a foolish man's heart. 'We are in Apache territory,' she said. 'In the land of Victorio.' That's when she pulled on the reins, slowed the buckboard, and looked me square in the eye. Need I tell you that I am not one to fold on a big hand? So I told her straight out: Kate, I said, I would rather face Victorio, Nana and Ulzana rather than hear one more word from you about matrimony. Kate, bless her black heart, just lashed out with a fine, strong leg and sent me sprawling to the ground, kicked me right off the buckboard. Bidding me adieu, Kate slapped those reins and rode away."

"I guess you do not love her, Kate, I mean."

"Oh, that is where you are wrong, young man. I love Kate—in my own peculiar fashion."

"Then why won't you marry her?"

A fearsome cough racked Doc's body, and he pressed a white handkerchief to his lips. When the cough subsided, I saw a spot of blood staining the fabric.

"Do you think," he asked, "that your father would sell me a horse? I have money, double eagles."

"Not a horse, but maybe a mule," I said.

"I owe you a great deal, young man. How may I ever repay you?"

Shaking my head, I told Doc Holliday that he did not owe me anything. I explained that feeding a hungry wayfarer was a tremendous mitzvah. Doc liked the word and repeated it several times. "Maybe someday, I can do a mitzvah for you," he said.

I invited Doc down to Jeremiah and Keturah's farm to spend the night. Side by side, we curled up under the wagon. I shared my blanket with him.

Right before sunrise, when the air became still, when the landscape went from black to silver-blue, Doc burst into another fit of coughing that racked his lank body like a storm. We were unable to get back to sleep.

Doc swallowed eagerly from his flask. "Back home in Valdosta, Georgia, I had a cousin, Martha Ann; I called her Mattie. She was, is, a fine young lady. I was young then, but oh, how I loved her. We lived right down the road from each other, and I saw Cousin Mattie practically every day. She was a quiet little girl, serious, not the frivolous Southern belle you hear so much about.

"One day Martha Ann told me that she had converted to Catholicism. We were raised as strict Methodists. I knew then what I had to do, and I did it."

"And what was that, Doc?"

"I asked Martha Ann to instruct me in the faith. I was sure that if I shared her religious passion, she would eventually love me, eventually be mine. Martha Ann said that she could not be my teacher. No, she sent me to a priest for proper lessons. I was baptized right and proper. Oh, how proud Cousin Mattie was as she stood at my baptism. Her face glowed. And my heart was full. We would be married in church; we would live a fine and upstanding life together."

Another cough, actually a series of coughs, seized Doc's body. He was a tall man, at least six feet in height, but he was thin, painfully so, and when his body shuddered I saw the pale skin of his face stretch against the bones, and his head became like a skull.

"What is wrong, Doc?"

He continued to cough and shake. I put my hand on his shoulder, but Doc shook me off, saying, "Don't touch. It's contagious."

"What is it?"

"I'm a lunger, son. You know what that means?"

I shook my head.

"Tuberculosis, contracted from my dear sweet mother. My life will be short, and you can be sure, brutal." He wiped a spray of blood off his fingers and continued. "A week after my baptism, Mattie left Valdosta. She wrote me a note telling me that she was going to be married."

"Oh, Doc, how terrible for you."

"No, there was no other man. You see, I had under-estimated Mattie's piety, her spiritual perfection. I had become Catholic so I could have Martha Ann as my own. Martha Ann had become Catholic so she could have God as her own. Martha Ann is now Sister Mary Melanie of St. Vincent's Convent; she is a nun, a Sister of Mercy."

"I'm sorry, Doc."

"I write to her every single week. I tell her everything. Well, not everything. I never told her about Dallas; that is where I killed my first man. I was practicing the art of dentistry at the time, and my patient, I do not recall his name, became somewhat irate over my skills. I shot my patient. Most unethical, but believe me, he deserved it. Besides, that wisdom tooth he had, it was badly infected, and it would have killed him sooner or later—at least I think it would have. After that, it was Fort Griffin, where I killed three blue-bellies at a poker table. They accused me of cheating. Now maybe I was and maybe I was not, but such vicious slurs cannot be left unchallenged. Killed Charlie White in

New Mexico. I believe that was over an insult to my honor. And then in Deadwood, with the aid of my friend and business colleague, Wyatt Earp, we went up against Joe Lighthorse. Why are you looking at me like that?"

"You are so casual, Doc. About killing, I mean."

"They all deserved it, son. Besides, you are missing my point, and that is: after cousin Mattie became a nun, I turned into what I am now."

"And what is that?"

"A sinner."

"But why?"

"Because she left me. I loved her—God, I still love her—and she abandoned me."

Doc's fine linen shirt was drenched in sweat, plastered to his skin. He took a small green bottle from his coat pocket, pulled off the cork stopper and took a long pull of a clear liquid. "Laudanum," he said, "the only way I can get any sleep these days."

Right before falling asleep, Doc whispered, "There are no words for this life."

A few minutes later, Doc Holliday was sleeping, his right hand resting heavily on his Colt Peacemaker. Doc was always ready for a fight. I suspect that his dreams must have been particularly violent, because he kept twitching in his sleep, moaning and yelping like a sick dog.

Chapter 15

—·· Shooters and Looters ··—

What a strange Shabbos: meeting the aristocratic and austere Doc Holliday in the dark, feeding him, befriending him, then listening to his tortured tale of love.

"Ariel, bist de du? Ariel, bist de du?"—Ariel, are you here? Ariel, are you here? Rebecca whispered.

"Yes, yes," I answered, "and we have a guest."

"I thought I heard voices." Yawning, Rebecca climbed down from the carriage and peeked at us. Doc and I crawled from beneath the wagon. I introduced my sister to Doc.

He bowed extravagantly and said, "Your beauty exceeds your dear brother's kindness."

Rebecca curtsied and studied our visitor. "Holliday, Doc Holliday…" Rebecca mused. "Have I not read about you in the newspapers?"

"Perhaps," replied Doc genially, "but you must not trust anything published by those rogues. They are notorious liars."

I explained that Doc was on his way to Tombstone. My sister's eyes lit up. "Tombstone, oh, how I long to see a real town, houses, stores." Gleefully, she asked, "Is it very, very big?"

"Big and getting bigger. Must be over twenty saloons by now. Though a delicate young lady such as yourself, I am sure, has no use for such dens of iniquity."

"Jews," asked Rebecca hopefully, "are there any Jews in Tombstone?"

"Jews in Tombstone," Doc mused, "It's been a while, but let me ponder a moment...You know, Mr. Schwartz, he runs a fine haberdashery. I'll wager he is a Jew. Now that I think about it, I recall that Mr. Schwartz had a most peculiar object on his store—a cylinder nailed to the doorpost that had some foreign writing on it. Someone told me it was of Hebrew origin."

"A mezuzah," cried Rebecca breathlessly. "Oh, Ariel, do you hear, there's a mezuzah in Tombstone! You must tell Papa that we have to go there. Maybe we'll even find a minyan for your bar mitzvah."

"What's that?" asked Doc.

I explained how important a minyan was for observant Jews and that my bar mitzvah, my coming of age, was next Shabbos.

"And Papa must find a minyan for Ariel," Rebecca insisted. "He simply has to."

◎ ◎ ◎

Later that morning, I explained to Papa who Doc was. Well, not *exactly* who Doc Holliday was. I did not mention all the gunfights he had been involved in. I simply explained that he was a lost and hungry traveler whom I had helped. I felt guilty for not telling Papa that Doc was a notorious pistoleer, but I did not want to scare Papa. There was no purpose in alarming anyone. Besides, I reasoned, Doc Holliday was my friend. He liked the word "mitzvah."

Keturah and Jeremiah gazed Doc's way suspiciously. Keturah whispered into Mama's ear, and soon enough Mama murmured to me in Yiddish that Doc sounded like a real shtarker—a tough guy. I could not argue.

Feeding Doc, Mama laid disapproving eyes on his two strapped-down pistols. Doc, a fastidious man, had shined the black leather holsters to a gleaming sheen.

Doc tried to charm Mama. "This, my dear lady, is the finest stew I have ever tasted."

"Cholent, it is called cholent."

"A rose by any other name. It is excellent, and you should go into business. You could make a fortune in Tombstone."

"Maybe you should take those guns off when you eat. It is not polite," Mama remonstrated.

Doc gazed at Mama with those pale blue eyes. How many men would dare say such a thing to him? Laying down his plate of cholent, Doc started to unbuckle his holster.

Just beyond the rise leading to the farm, we noticed that a wall of dust was floating towards us.

"You expecting company?" Doc asked.

Jeremiah shook his head.

Papa studied the cloud. "Perhaps it is the Indians."

Doc checked the bullets in his pistols. "No, sir—I mean, Rabbi." Doc was polite and respectful to Papa. "No Injun would ever make that much dust. They might be many things, but stupid is not one of them."

I scrambled to the top of the bluff. Five riders were approaching the farm. They were white men. But they were like no men I had ever seen.

"Strange men, Doc," I called out. "Their clothing is animal hides, and there are brushes hanging round their necks."

Serenely, Doc said, "There might be trouble." He looked around. "I want the women inside. Jeremiah, you too, in the cabin, and position yourself at the window."

"I don't shoot very straight," Jeremiah stammered.

"If need be, I'll do the killing," said Doc benignly. "You just do your best to look dangerous, like some redneck assassin with no regard for human life."

"And me?" asked Papa.

"My dear Rabbi," Doc answered equably, "you comfort the women. And if I should fall, I would greatly appreciate a proper burial. Psalm twenty-three is a particular favorite of mine."

I ran to the wagon, reached into my bag and pulled out the Walker. Stunned, Papa looked at me. "Ariel, it is Shabbos."

"Papa," I said, "this is a matter of life and death."

"But you… you are just a child," Papa pleaded.

"No, Papa, no longer. I am almost bar mitzvah."

Papa's expression fell. He looked at me as if I were suddenly a stranger. I realized that more and more I felt oysgegrient—more un-green—every day.

Doc studied the gun in my hand. "All right, son, hop under that wagon. Keep your eye on me. If I slap leather, you start shooting. Do not worry about your aim. You will not be able to hit anything, not the way that machine kicks. So just keep firing, and make lots of noise."

"Noise?"

"A great deal of noise," he said patiently.

Urgently I asked, "Who are they, Doc?"

"Scalphunters. The devil's own."

We all got into position. Sitting in a ladderback chair, Doc calmly continued to eat Mama's cholent. I took comfort from Doc's confidence. But my throat tightened as the five scalphunters came riding into the farm. I gaped at them; clad entirely in leather and hide, they appeared like men from another world, a world of voracious hunters and yellow-eyed animals.

The brushes around their necks were human scalps. They wore them proudly, like trophies. More scalps hung from their belts and from their saddles. A dark and foul odor hung in the air. It smelled like a slaughterhouse.

Skin black with filth, eyes shining from red-rimmed sockets, they rode up to Doc and watched him as he calmly continued to eat. He dabbed lightly at his lips with the lace handkerchief. The leader of the scalphunters, his red hair tangled and crusted with filth, addressed Doc.

"Smells good, that stew."

"Cholent."

"What's that?"

"It is cholent. Quite distinct from ordinary stew."

Red Hair looked askance at Doc.

Doc said, "Business good, gentlemen?"

Red Hair grinned. His teeth were black stumps. "Business is real good. We got a passel of Apache scalps. Governor of Chihuahua is payin' fifty dollars for a buck's scalp, twenty-five for a squaw or young'n."

"It takes courageous men to hunt down Apaches."

"We're real brave." They all chuckled.

"Yes," continued Doc, "a few years back I did some scouting for General Crook. Went after that old killer Nana. We tracked them, Al Sieber and I, over a thousand miles, through Arizona, New Mexico, Texas, right on into Old Mexico. You know how many we killed?"

"How many?" asked the second rider. His face was a living canvas of pagan tattoos.

"Not one. No, sir, we did not see one Apache in three months of march. What we did see were fifty-four dead settlers: men, women and children."

Doc drummed the fingers of his right hand on his thigh. I sensed that something was about to happen.

"What are you implying, friend?" said Red Hair.

"I suspect that you and I, sir, will never be friends. So please call me by my proper name."

"And what that might be?"

"John Henry Holliday."

"Doc Holliday?" said Red Hair.

Doc nodded.

The scalphunters visibly stiffened in their saddles.

"I am not implying anything," Doc continued with barely disguised contempt, "I am saying it straight out: trash like you could not go up against an Apache child, much less a raiding buck. Those scalps are Mexican. Maybe even white folks. I am sure you do not discriminate."

Red Hair's hand twitched, but Doc was fast, so fast I did not even see his hands move. Suddenly, his twin Peacemakers were clear of their holsters and pointed right at Red Hair.

"You can't kill all of us," Red Hair challenged with a mad grin.

"Why not?" Doc's voice was cold and distant. He would kill, and he would not feel any remorse.

The smile vanished from the scalphunter's lips.

I pulled back the hammer on the Walker. The dry click seemed unnaturally loud. All the scalphunters turned and looked at me. The door to Jeremiah's shack swung open, and I could not believe my eyes. Standing with the shotgun in hand was Rebecca.

"Doc," said Rebecca, "which one should I shoot first?"

Doc did not look happy. "Step back, young lady."

Red Hair stared at Rebecca. Licking his lips he said, "One of your lady friends Doc? You got fine taste."

"Let me kill him first," said Rebecca. She aimed the shotgun at Red Hair. My sister's finger tightened, turned snow white on the double trigger.

Red Hair paled and lifted his hands into the air.

"Ain't lookin' for no trouble. If we ride out, Doc, you swear not to shoot us in the back?"

Doc nodded.

My sister said, "Please let me shoot him, Doc. How dare this sheygitz trash insult me in such a manner?"

"Doc?" pleaded Tattoo nervously.

Doc chuckled. "Much as I'd love to see the young lady blow your skull to hell and back, well, ride on. I will not countenance any back-shooting—even if you sons of Satan do so richly deserve it."

Whipping their horses heartlessly, the scalphunters galloped away. Doc stood in the path of Rebecca's aim, making sure that she would not shoot.

"What happened in there, Miss Rebecca?"

"Jeremiah fainted. There was no one else to take his place."

"You should not have made an appearance. You should not have let those men see you."

"Why not?"

"Because they are shooters and looters; they steal white women for sale to the great haciendas down in Old Mexico. And you are too beautiful to escape their evil designs."

Rebecca blushed, lowered the shotgun. Doc turned and stared; soon the scalphunters became just a mote in the eye.

"Yes, far too beautiful ever to be forgotten," he added bleakly to no one in particular.

◎　◎　◎

Doc bought one of our mules, and, before riding off to Tombstone, scrawled something on his business card and handed it to me.

"If you ever need me, just show this card to anyone in Tombstone, and I will find you."

"Doc?"

"What is it, son?"

"You just performed a tremendous mitzvah."

Grinning, Doc tipped his hat to all of us and rode off. Rebecca sighed like one of the damsels in her novels. Mama fixed her with a cold glare.

I bid goodbye to the elegant killer, expecting never to see him again, but as fate would have it, before too long, Doc Holliday performed another great mitzvah for me, a mitzvah that would undoubtedly make the sages of the Talmud smile in their heavenly beis midrash.

That night, just as I was about to go to sleep, Papa said, "Ariel, I have decided."

"Decided what, Papa?"

"Tomorrow, after we help with the chores, we will pack up and leave."

"Leave for where?"

"Tombstone. We leave for Tombstone, where we will gather a minyan for your bar mitzvah."

I wrapped my arms around Papa's waist and held him for a long moment.

Chapter 16

—· Circles ·—

The next morning, as I was feeding Jeremiah's chickens, I was halted in my tracks by the broken noise of sobbing. Mama came running over.

"Mama, Mama, what's wrong?"

Other than a wail, I got no answer.

"Mama, please calm down, what is it?"

"Rebecca, it's Rebecca," she cried.

"What about Rebecca?"

"Gone."

"Gone?"

"Oy, oy!" Mama was reeling, her expression filled with that scrambled gaze of bewilderment and terror that can only live in the heart of a mother.

"Mama, what do you mean gone? Gone where?"

It was no use. Mama was completely hysterical. She began hiccupping. I ran back to the house.

"Rebecca went down to the stream to get water," said Papa.

"And she didn't come back," added Keturah.

"We best hurry," said Jeremiah.

We all ran over the slope that led to the creek. There we saw the wooden bucket lying on its side in the sparkling water. I discovered Rebecca's blue silk hair ribbon on the ground, trampled in the mud. Jeremiah leaned down and examined the wet soil.

"Riders," he said.

"How many?" I asked.

"Looks to be five."

"The scalphunters?" I offered.

Jeremiah gravely nodded. "The way they was lookin' at your sister, I wouldn't be surprised if'n they come back and stole her."

"We don't have the money to pay a ransom," I said.

"They ain't lookin' for no ransom from you folks. They know you ain't got two coins to your name. No, as Doc told you, they steal white women and sell them as kitchen slaves across the Rio Grande. It's a vigorous business. Them rich Mexicans pay gold coins and no questions asked."

My stomach dropped.

Keturah clapped a hand to her mouth.

"For what I feared has overtaken me; what I dreaded has come upon me," Papa quoted from the book of Job. His voice was thick with dread, thick with love.

◎　◎　◎

As Jeremiah helped me saddle his horse, a chestnut roan, he kept giving me worried looks.

"You shouldn't ought to do this, Ariel."

"I have no choice."

"I'd come with you, but…" His voice trailed off.

"No, you have to stay, I understand."

"Say y'do manage to catch up with them heathen scalp-hunters. What're you gonna do then?"

I lifted my jacket, displaying the Walker.

"How many shells y'got?"

"Six… I think."

Jeremiah walked into the cabin and came out with a Winchester rifle.

"You take this here rifle, button. Real fine at long distance, and that's how I recommend huntin' these varmints."

I thanked him and took the weapon. Jeremiah dropped a dozen cartridges into my jacket pocket. They rattled like coins.

Papa and Mama came up to me as Jeremiah hoisted me up into the saddle.

"Ariel…" said Papa mournfully.

"Do not worry, it will be all right," I told him.

Mama handed me a feed bag; I hung it over the pommel.

"Bread and potato kugel, that's all I have ready."

"Thank you, Mama."

"What can one little boy do against five Cossacks?" Mama asked in an anxious voice.

"King David defeated Goliath with one small pebble," I replied. I tried to sound brave, but my voice wavered like a thin sheet of parchment in the wind.

"Save my tochter," implored Mama—save my daughter.

"I should maybe come with you," Papa said.

"No, Papa, you can hardly even ride a horse. You would just slow me up. And we do not have a great deal of time. Pray, Papa, pray that one of the Lamed Vovniks helps me rescue Rebecca." Papa nodded, a gentle creature, pious and holy, but quite defenseless against evil.

He motioned for me to lean down. He placed his hands over my head and intoned:

May God bless you and protect you. May God cause His face to shine upon you and be gracious to you. May He raise His countenance to you and establish peace for you.

There was a heavy silence as Papa's eyes sought mine. I kissed Papa's hand.

"My son," cried Papa, "my son!"

◎ ◎ ◎

The tracks left by the scalphunters were clear and vivid, a map of their journey. These men were brazen, not at all concerned about being followed. Every part of my body was crying out Rebecca's name. All she wanted—all my sister ever wanted—was to attend an ice-cream social.

I rode all day, right through the devastating heat of the afternoon. Even with my hat on, the sun beat down upon me with relentless fury. The tracks led south, toward Old Mexico. My muscles were sore, the backs of my thighs were burning and the stirrups ground through my thin cotton trousers, rubbing bloody patches into my calves.

I knew that I had to conserve water and food, so I only took little sips from my canteen once every hour. However, even with being so careful, by the time the late afternoon shadows gathered and stretched across the desert, my canteen was almost empty. Swollen and dry, my tongue felt like a piece of shoe leather in my mouth. I had to find water for myself and for the horse.

◎ ◎ ◎

A dark fortress of clouds moved in from the northwest, an angry wedge of steel gray. Before I knew it darkness fell, and there I was in the middle of an endless dry plain. As I built a fire, the desert wind picked up, and suddenly I was shivering with cold. Arizona: scorching days, freezing nights. Mindful of Jeremiah's horse and of the Biblical injunction to feed your animal before yourself, I gave the horse the last of my water, and then the last of my food. If I did not find water tomorrow there was a good chance I would die. And if I died, what would become of Rebecca?

The wind grew stronger, more violent, and soon I was caught in a savage dust storm. The wind howled crazily and blew fine grains of sand up my nostrils. I hunched down into my jacket, covering my face as best I could, protecting my eyes from the stinging wind and grit. The fierce storm blew all night, roaring like an ocean in my ears. Wherever my flesh was exposed, it felt as if pins and razor blades were striking it. My throat was so tight that I could barely swallow; tears leaked from my eyes.

All night long, I shivered in my blanket, drifting off to sleep for just a few precious minutes at a time. I was assaulted by dream-like images, visions that made no sense.

I saw circles in the sand.

Endless circles in an endless desert.

When sunrise finally came, I groped my way back to consciousness, lifted my face to the welcome sun and felt its heat warm my skin. The morning was as clear as glass.

And the scalphunters' tracks were gone, blown away by the dust storm. I had no idea which way to ride. Where had the scalphunters gone?

I was lost, and time was quickly running out.

I decided to continue south into old Mexico, straight towards the Chiricahua Mountains. Perhaps, with luck, I would manage to pick up their trail. Perhaps, with luck, I would locate water in the foothills.

The mountains did not seem to be very far away, but hour after hour, I pushed on, and the mountains appeared no nearer. Like ghostly apparitions, they kept receding. One moment they were tantalizingly close, almost within the touch of my finger tips, and then, abruptly, they were gone, oozing away like mist.

The sun climbed higher in the sky, burned mercilessly.

The horse weakened; I could feel his body quivering, his muscles twitching, and so I climbed down and led him by the reins.

The sun was burning the world white. The air was heavy and harsh, difficult to breathe.

Circles.

Abruptly, it came to me.

There is a story in the Talmud about Honi the Circlemaker. Honi was a holy sage who lived at the time of the First Temple, the temple built by King Solomon. A famine swept Israel, and the people came to Honi and asked him to pray for rain. Honi began to pray, but rain did not fall. What did Honi do? He drew a circle in the ground and planted himself within it. "Master of the Universe," he said, "Your children have turned to me to pray for rain on their behalf, and I swear by Your great name that I will not leave this circle until you have mercy on your children and send rain." As soon as Honi finished, rain began to come down.

Parched and dizzy, I drew a circle in the desert floor with the heel of my shoe and stood within the circle. The horse looked at me as if questioning my sanity.

"Master of the Universe," I said, "I am not Honi the Circlemaker. As a matter of fact, I am just Ariel, son of Rabbi Shmuel, but I beg, I beseech you, send rain. My sister is in trouble and I am the only one who can help her. I will not move from this circle until you give me water."

Nothing.

The sky remained perfectly blue, like the throat of a peacock.

"I mean it," I said, "I will not move until you send water."

Still nothing.

I sat down, stared at the distant mountains. The sun, a golden ball of fire, was bathing me in fire. My head ached; it felt as if a steel spike were going right through my skull. My vision turned blurry, and stars seemed to be exploding right before my eyes. One galaxy right after the other. So this is what it feels like to die, I thought.

Then the world disappeared.

※

Chapter 17

—·Riding with the Apache ·—

Something cool and wet moved across my lips. I opened my mouth, water splashed, slid down my throat. I swallowed greedily, gulped one cool mouthful after another.

As if from a great distance a voice called, "Ariel... Ariel..."

I opened my eyes.

Lozen smiled at me. Standing beside her was Victorio. He was in full war paint, black and vermilion stripes bisecting the planes of his face. His skin gleamed with grease, and his hair, black as night, fell in a long wave past his shoulders. He carried a Henry rifle and a bow and quiver of arrows, and two pistols were thrust in his belt.

Behind him, four Apache warriors, also in war paint, were mounted on ponies; they were grinning at me.

Sitting up, I became dizzy and fell back. The Apaches chuckled, deeply amused. Lozen supported me with her arm, gave me more water. I had never tasted anything so delicious in all my life.

"Lozen," I said, "What are you—where have you been?"

"I went on my vision quest, Ariel. It is the Apache custom. It is how a girl becomes a woman. And on my vision quest, I found my power. I found it on the sacred mountain."

"You mean you had a bar mitzvah?"

"An Apache bar mitzvah," she said, eyes twinkling.

"I'm sorry I wasn't there, to help you celebrate."

"It is something we do alone, Ariel. On the mountain, I fasted for three days and three nights. Prayed for three days and three nights. And I saw you, Ariel. I saw you in a circle. I saw the circle was on fire. I saw my power. And so after I came down from the sacred mountain, I went to the farm, and they told me what happened."

I jumped to my feet and deliriously shouted, "It worked. It worked. It is a miracle! A true miracle!"

Lozen frowned.

"My circle, Lozen. It worked. I prayed for rain. I prayed for water and God sent you. It is just like Honi the Circlemaker. Have I ever told you about Honi? Oh, no, I have not gotten to that one with you. But God sent you, Lozen, God sent you to save me."

"Ussen sent me. My power sent me."

There was no time to argue about religion.

"Lozen, my sister has been stolen."

"We know, and we know the men who did it."

"You do?"

"Bad men. Very bad."

"Can we catch them? Can we rescue Rebecca?"

Lozen turned and looked at her brother, deferring to his authority.

"Victorio?" I said.

Here was the most feared Apache in the New Mexico and Arizona territories. He nodded a mute greeting, stared at me, dark eyes flecked with silver, bottomless eyes. Here was a leader, a natural-born leader of men. Grand and remote, his presence was powerful, and I felt as if I were meeting a prince or a king.

"I am proud to meet the great Victorio," I said.

He continued gazing at me.

Nervously, I continued, "Our tradition, the tradition of my tribe, is to present a gift to a great leader."

Victorio waited.

I went to my horse, reached into the saddlebag and took out my siddur, my prayer book. I presented it to Victorio. He held the small volume in his hand, opened its pages and looked at the Hebrew print.

"What do the tracks say?" he asked. His voice was deep.

"These are prayers and words of wisdom from our holy men, words from before the beginning of time. These are words that have helped keep my people alive through every war during our long history."

Victorio caressed the soft pages, tucked the leather-bound volume in his belt. He issued what sounded like a string of commands. The Apache warriors sawed on their reins and galloped off.

"Where are they going?" I asked.

"Keep eye on trail of the scalphunters," Victorio replied.

"I did not take enough water," I said, feeling stupid.

"Plenty of water right here," said Victorio.

I looked around. All I saw was sand, sky, clumps of cholla cactus, and distant mountains.

"There is no water here."

Lozen led me to a low cluster of brush so thick with barbed spines that it looked like white fur. Using her knife as a shovel, Lozen dug right underneath the plants. After a few minutes the sand turned damp with moisture. With more digging, something miraculous happened: a tiny bit of water seeped up from beneath the ground. I tasted the water; it was gritty.

"Wait," said Lozen.

She took the hem of her skirt and laid it in the bottom of the bowl she had dug. The fabric acted as a strainer as pure water rose up, warm but pleasing.

"Hebrew Kid has much to learn," Lozen said, looking at Victorio. The great warrior grinned. He spoke to Lozen in Apache and galloped away.

"Does Victorio know where my sister is?"

"He will find her."

"And then what will happen?"

"War."

◎ ◎ ◎

We rode for hours. I told Lozen about Honi the Circlemaker. She liked the story and asked if there were any more.

"Lozen, are we going to rescue Rebecca?"

"Tell me more about the Circlemaker."

"You want to hear about Honi because he had power?"

Lozen nodded.

"All right. This is another story from the same book. A book called Ta'anis—fasts."

"Fasts? You do this too?"

"Yes, but just for one day."

"Why?"

"So God will send rain."

"Jews do this, Ariel?"

"In our homeland, long ago, yes. We also fast to remember great defeats in war."

"It is better to forget defeats."

"We remember them."

"Why?"

"Because a great defeat means that God is punishing us and we must do t'shuvah, repentance. We must say that we are sorry, beg for forgiveness."

"This is what your God wants?"

I nodded.

Lozen thought this over for a long moment. Finally, she said, "Does your God forgive you?"

"Only if we are sincere. If we are lying, God knows it."

"Ariel?"

"Yes?"

"You are a good member of your tribe?"

"You mean, am I a good Jew?"

She nodded.

"I try."

"Your father, mother, sister, good Jews?"

"I think so. Yes, they are, very good Jews."

"Then why does your God let scalphunters steal your sister?"

I said nothing.

"No answer, Ariel?"

"There is a master plan, Lozen. It is God's plan. We do not know what it is. We have no idea how He arranges events in the world. We can only trust; we can only hope that good will emerge from bad."

"So if Rebecca is sold into slavery or if she dies, you will accept this as part of your God's plan?"

"I must do everything I can to save her, Lozen. I must not just give up."

"But you will accept God's judgment?"

I nodded.

"Happily?"

"No, with grief."

◙ ◙ ◙

I told Lozen another story about Honi.

"One day Honi was walking along the road when he saw a man planting a carob tree. Honi said to the man, 'In how many years will this tree that you are planting bear fruit?' Answered the man, 'It should take about seventy years.' Honi said to him, 'Are you certain that you will be alive in seventy years?' The man explained to Honi, 'I found a world filled with carob trees. Those trees were planted for the benefit of future generations. Just as my ancestors planted carob trees for my benefit, so too must I plant for the benefit of my children and grandchildren.'

"Honi sat down and ate his afternoon meal. When he finished eating, he fell into a deep sleep. God caused a cave to form around Honi, and this is how he remained asleep for many nights. When he finally awoke, he saw someone picking carobs from the tree that had just been planted. Honi said to the man, 'Are you the one who planted this tree?' The man answered, 'No, that was my grandfather.' Honi realized what must have happened; he understood that he had been asleep for seventy years."

"A good story," said Lozen.

"It's not the end," I said.

"Honi then went back to his old house and asked, 'Is the son of Honi still alive?' The people said to him, 'His son is no longer alive, but his grandson is still living.' He then cried out, 'I am Honi the Circlemaker! I have been asleep for seventy years!' But his family did not believe him. He went to the beis midrash, the school where he used to teach, and proclaimed: 'I am Honi the Circlemaker and I have been asleep for seventy years.' Just like his family, the rabbis and students did not believe him, and they did not give him the respect he was due. Honi was very sad. He had no family; he had no friends. And so he begged for mercy, asking God to put an end to his life."

"What happened?"

"Honi the Circlemaker died. God took his life, just as he had pleaded."

Lozen wiped her eyes with the heel of her hand.

"Lozen, are you crying?"

"Something in my eye," she replied, annoyed.

Lozen nudged her horse and rode ahead.

◎　◎　◎

Several hours later, Victorio's warriors returned. They were encrusted with a fine coat of yellow dust and looked like part of the terrible landscape. Briefly, they conferred with Lozen; she nodded her head.

"What, what is it?" I asked.

"Your sister. They have found Rebecca."

"Thank God. Is she all right?"

Lozen dismounted, checked the hooves of her horse, and pried loose several tiny stones.

"Is she alive?" I demanded.

Lozen did not answer.

"Lozen, is Rebecca alive?" I repeated. "You have to tell me."

For an answer, her eyes slid away from mine; for the first time since I had known Lozen, she refused to meet my gaze. My heart was having convulsions. Hot tears pooled in my eyes. I trembled and shook. I had failed to rescue my sister. How was I ever going to face Mama and Papa; how was I ever going to live with myself? A morass of helplessness and despair moved through my body.

Rebecca must be dead.

Chapter 18
—· To Fight and To Die ·—

The earth and sky were one, a silver bowl. Lozen gave
me a long enfolding gaze. I felt as if her eyes were
wings: dark, shining wings that spanned the length of the
desert. Oh, if only my friends back in Europe could see me
now; instead of learning Talmud, studying the ancient laws
of Judaism, I was riding with an Apache war party, riding to
save my sister's life. But too late. Too late. An assault of
tears made my whole body tremble uncontrollably.

"She is alive," said Lozen.

I looked at the Apache maiden, not quite believing what
I had just heard. Did Lozen just say that Rebecca was…?

"Alive," she repeated.

"But if she is… why did you…?"

"There are more than five men now," she said.

"More than five scalphunters?"

Lozen nodded and explained, "Vaqueros from the great
hacienda have joined them; they are to buy slaves for the
house."

It took a moment for this to sink in. Lozen continued, "There are more men than Apache. We will be outnumbered. It is too dangerous. They have many more guns than we do."

"I don't care, Lozen."

"Dangerous for Rebecca too."

"You mean they will kill her?"

"They are evil men. Who knows what they will do?"

"We have to try. I can't just give up."

"Victorio will not tell warriors to fight such a battle."

The long low clouds in the west looked as if they were on fire. Roosting birds clamored in the brush. A lizard slid across a gray boulder. The sun was sinking, turning the horizon to blood.

"But he is your leader," I entreated. "He is the great Victorio. All he has to do is order his warriors to fight."

She shook her head. I did not understand the Apache people. "A true chief does not make his braves fight when warriors do not have enough men or weapons," she said. "It is not the way of the Apache."

Stunned, speechless, I stood rooted to the spot. It took me a moment to understand what Lozen was saying. It took me a moment to comprehend the terrible thing she was telling me.

"You mean that you will just leave my sister where she is, let her be sold into slavery?" I stammered.

"It is how it is."

"No. It does not have to be this way."

"But it is what it is."

"I thought Apache believed in honor."

"It is not honor to die for nothing."

I gaped at her. "What did you say? My sister is not nothing, Lozen. She is a person, a human being just like you."

My heart was careening as I spoke, because I knew that Victorio and his warriors had already made up their minds, and it made no difference what I said.

"Ariel's sister is not of our tribe."

Thunderstruck, I could only stare at her. "Is that what this is about? If my sister were Apache, would your braves fight for her?"

Lozen simply nodded and said, "Would you fight to save an Apache girl from slavery?"

"Of course," I replied without hesitation.

"Why?"

"Because it is the right thing to do; because God commands us to protect the weak from the strong, the innocent from the evil."

Lozen kneeled and drew circles in the sand; circles within circles; wheels inside wheels. Her raven hair fell at right angles to her nose. I was mesmerized by the loops, dazzled by the intricate drawings.

In the days of the Temple, the unmarried daughters of Israel would dance in elaborate circles.

The Kabbalah explains that the dancing circle symbolizes God's universe that has no end and no beginning. The good and the righteous were promised endless spiritual rewards, and at the time, each girl in the circle was able to use her finger to point to God's revelation.

"I will fight with you, Ariel," whispered Lozen softly. "I will fight and die with you." At that moment, with the sun falling, the harsh shadows stretching into infinity, Lozen and I ceased to be children.

Chapter 19

—· Forever ·—

Lozen and I rode hard all night. When I asked her where Victorio and the other warriors had gone, she just gestured to the far horizon. She said nothing more, as if it no longer mattered, as if the different paths she and her brother had chosen were of no importance.

"Doesn't your brother want you to stay with him? Does he really want you to go and fight, especially in a battle that we will probably lose?"

"Victorio wants me to be loyal to what I believe," she said, "and my loyalty, Ariel, is to you."

I quickly hauled in the reins and pulled to a stop. I felt my blood beating. Lozen tugged on her reins, turned and looked at me, nailed me with her most penetrating gaze, and I saw that her eyes were infinitely deep, opening like a tunnel into another universe. My soul was tumbling, heartsick. I was forcing Lozen to do battle against those terrible scalphunters, as wicked, as obsessed and steely as the land that had bred them.

"And I am loyal to you, Lozen," I replied.

That's something that most people don't understand about the Apache. Once they choose a side, they stick with their choice; their sense of honor and loyalty is heroic; no matter what happens, they will not abandon you, no matter how terrible the odds.

"Hurry," she said in the leaden stillness. "We must get to Apache Canyon before the sun comes up."

"Lozen?"

"Yes?"

"Nothing."

We looked at each another for a moment. I wanted to thank her, to tell her that I had never met anyone like her in my whole life, but I knew not to say such things. The Apache did not believe in saying everything that they were thinking, especially when you were saying nice things about another person. They believed that silence sometimes said more than all the words on your tongue. To compliment an Apache, especially an Apache maiden, was almost bad manners.

I think Lozen understood perfectly what was going through my mind, because she flashed me a dazzling smile, then whipped her pony. "Hurry, Ariel, we must hurry." We rode, both our horses breaking into a liquid gallop.

We seemed to fly through the wasteland, through the moon-drenched desert.

Indigo night against a black terrain. With my face open to the bitter cold of the clear night, I could follow the path of the heavenly bodies. I felt as if I knew the stars, the sweep of galaxies, as if I had been among them my whole life. In the pale flood of moonlight, Lozen and I turned into seraphim, skimming across the harsh wilderness, and all the wonder of what Lozen said, of what I felt, settled in my throat like a cooing dove.

◎ ◎ ◎

We came to the foothills of Apache Canyon half an hour before sunrise. Lozen led me up a narrow game trail to the summit of the canyon. There on a flat expanse of limestone, a ragged plateau, we finally rested. As soon as we stopped moving, a chill came over me, and I started to shake, my teeth chattered uncontrollably. Lozen wrapped her blanket around me.

"Don't you need it?" I said.

"I am Apache," replied Lozen as if that alone explained everything.

"What are we doing here?" I asked after a few minutes.

"Soon you will see," she said.

"Lozen?"

"Yes, Ariel?"

"Do you really think we're going to die?"

Lozen calmly said, "I have prepared my death song."

"Papa will say Kaddish for me. Kaddish, I suppose that's our death song, though it never mentions death."

"What does your death song say?"

"It praises God."

"You praise your God when you die?"

"Yes."

"Why?"

"Because that's the moment when we are most likely to be angry with him, to reject him. The Kaddish reminds us to love God even in the face of death."

Lozen chuckled.

"What's funny?"

"We are so different, yet so much is the same. My death song also praises Ussen." Lozen ripped a thin strip of cloth from the hem of her skirt and started to clean the barrel of her revolver. "It will be good to die with you, Ariel."

"Can we try not to die, Lozen?"

Lozen smiled. Her fine white teeth shone like pearls.

"You will have to tell me what to do," I said timidly. "I have never fought in a battle before."

"Just do what I tell you. I have learned everything I know from Victorio."

We both snatched a few restless minutes of sleep. In the dark before dawn, I was able to make out the delicate lines of Lozen's face, her smooth skin, like bronze.

"I trust you, Lozen."

"And I trust you."

"You once said that you would never trust a white-eye."

"You are not a white-eye, Ariel. You are a Jew, a member of a different tribe."

◎　◎　◎

The rising sun appeared, first a single line of quivering gold that turned to royal purple, then an immense orb hovering over the horizon.

"You see," whispered Lozen, "it is behind us."

I looked down into the canyon. There, the scalphunters and a group of Mexican vaqueros were sleeping by a dead campfire. Empty liquor jugs were scattered all about the canyon floor.

Then I saw Rebecca.

Her wrists were bound together, staked to the ground. Her dress was torn at the shoulder, and she was barefoot, her shoes taken from her so she would be unable to escape. I started to call her name, but Lozen clamped her palm over my mouth. She pressed her fingers to her lips, pointed to the sun, then gestured to the scalphunters' camp.

I was beginning to understand Lozen's battle plan.

I had Jeremiah's rifle and the Walker pistol. Lozen had a rifle and a brace of pistols, but she preferred to use her bow and arrows, traditional Apache weapons.

As the morning light oozed across the canyon floor, the scalphunters and vaqueros stirred, crawled out of their blankets, tugged on their boots. Grumbling and complaining, they went about their morning routine of building fires and boiling coffee. Some of the men roundly cursed their headaches, pulled out more bottles of liquor and began to drink. They were all heavily armed, each man a clanking arsenal of weapons.

Lozen and I had to strike while Rebecca was still down

in the canyon; we had to attack before the vaqueros spirited Rebecca away to Old Mexico to serve as a kitchen slave. Once they started to move, our very slim advantage of surprise would be lost.

We had to attack while the sun was at our backs.

We had to attack while the men were still half-asleep and disoriented.

There were a dozen men all together, outlaws and killers, shooters and looters, against Lozen and me: the Hebrew Kid and the Apache Maiden.

And Rebecca could not run. She would be stranded in the middle of the battlefield, trapped and defenseless.

But we had no choice.

Lozen pointed to the five scalphunters who were grouped together on the western edge of the camp.

Lozen's very substance, her every motion was now somehow transformed. Her body spoke a precise, martial tongue, a language reeking of knowledge and terrible experience. The warrior history of her people, the fearless Mimbres Apache, was in her every breath. As Torah was in my blood, war was in Lozen's.

"When, when should I shoot?" I stammered tensely.

"After my first arrow flies."

I nodded. My mouth was dry as desert sand, and a thick nugget, like a walnut, formed in my throat.

Lozen carefully laid out her quiver of arrows, neatly separated the shafts, and looked over her shoulder at the climbing sun.

"And now I will pray for our victory," she said. Eyes closed, on her knees, she chanted in Apache. When she finished, I asked her to translate.

In this world Ussen has power. This power He has granted me for the good of my people. This I see as one from a height sees in every direction. This I feel as though I held in my palms something that tingles. This power is mine to use.

Positioning myself at the edge of the ridge, I brought the rifle to my cheek and looked down the barrel. I would shoot Red Hair first. He was the leader. It was he who had probably hatched the plot to steal my sister and sell her into a life of slavery.

Cold sweat ran down my forehead, made mist of my vision and stung my eyes. I wiped my face clear with the back of my hand, but the sweat kept pouring down and soaking my shirt. Lozen plucked a red bandanna from her belt and tied it around my forehead. In spite of the fear, there were things I had to say.

"Lozen?"

"Sshh."

"Would you come to my bar mitzvah—if we get out of this alive?"

"Ariel, I have to tell you something, something important."

"What, what is it?"

"You can never be my husband," she said solemnly, "because you are not Apache. Are you angry with me?"

"No. Lozen. I'm not. Because the truth is, you can never be my wife because you are not Jewish."

"But our friendship, that will last forever, yes, Ariel?"

"Yes, forever," I agreed.

We gazed at each other for a long moment. I listened to the silence. It was a silence with a particular resonance. It was the sound of eternity.

Again, Lozen looked over her shoulder at the steadily climbing sun.

"It is time," she whispered.

Lozen rose to one knee, notched an arrow into her bow, pulled back the cord. The bow curved, and then—one of the Vaqueros stiffened, cried out, and pitched to the ground, an arrow buried in his chest.

But Lozen had not fired her arrow.

There was chaos in the camp below as more arrows—a world of arrows—poured into the camp. The Apache war cry, a piercing, terrifying ululation, filled the air.

Turning around, I saw that Victorio and his four warriors were positioned on a shelf behind us.

Steadily, with deadly accuracy, they fired arrows down into the canyon. The scalphunters and vaqueros tried to shoot back, tried to find their targets, but the blazing sun was in their eyes, blinding them, and their shots went wild, never coming close to any of us. They were shooting at enemies no more substantial than ghosts. For them, it must have seemed as if the very landscape had risen against them. Chaos reigned; the air of panic was palpable. The shrill discordant battle cry of the Apache sounded, even to my ears, like the voice of hell itself.

The last time my family had been attacked, back in Russia, I ran. I hid, cried and shivered like a frightened animal. No more. This time I was fighting back. The Russian authorities did not allow Jews to own guns; it was against the law. Here in America, everyone is allowed to own a weapon; everyone can defend his life against the inevitable evil that crouches at the door.

As if possessed of a will and life of its own, my finger squeezed the trigger, and, crying out in shock, Red Hair went sprawling in the churning dust. His blood, bright, glistening red and alive, pooled on the hard ground.

I had killed a man. And although Red Hair richly deserved to die, I felt sick; I felt hollow.

Unruffled and almost machinelike, Lozen snapped off one arrow after another. I could not tell if she hit anyone, because there were so many arrows singing in the air at the same time. I glanced over my shoulder and watched in awe as Victorio sent forth his arrows. The great war chief was able to launch three arrows in the air quicker than I could lever and fire three shells.

I could see men falling, men crawling and groaning, and men dying. Some of the dying scalphunters cried out for their mothers; several vaqueros prayed to their God. Many of the men simply cursed the devil and their luck. It was a choir of broken lamentations.

As all around her the ground turned into a battlefield, Rebecca cried, screamed, and begged this nightmare to end. I myself was in a half-daze, stunned by the noise and confusion, the acrid smell of gunpowder, yet aware that my mood was swinging between elation at the Apache bravery and the pure terror of battle.

Abruptly, it was all over. There they lay, more than a dozen bodies, corpses feathered with arrows. Victorio signaled his warriors to halt their lethal assault.

"Rebecca!" I cried. "Rebecca!"

My sister looked up at the sound of my voice.

"Ariel! Ariel!" shrieked Rebecca, and her thin body was racked with uncontrollable sobbing.

We clambered down to the floor of the canyon. As I approached Rebecca, I saw that her hair was filthy and matted, her wrists, tightly bound by rawhide straps, were raw and bleeding. I dropped my pistol and ran to her.

A corpse stirred.

He rolled over and placed the barrel of his pistol right up against Rebecca's temple.

Red Hair was still alive.

"I'll kill her!" he screamed.

The Apache froze in their tracks. I too stayed absolutely still, stared in bewildered horror.

"Unless you savages get gone right this very minute, I'll blow her brains out."

In the awful silence that followed, the hollow click of his gun's hammer echoed off the steep walls of the canyon.

❦

Chapter 20

—· End of the Journey ·—

Rebecca's eyes were wide with terror. Her body tilted away from Red Hair and his pistol, but he viciously jabbed her with the tip of the barrel, hissing, "Don't you move, Jew-girl, or I'll just put one in your brain and be done with it."

"Ariel," cried Rebecca. "Help me."

"Shut up!" howled Red Hair. "Now, this is what I want—"

Victorio unfolded like a flower, arm and wrist whipping, and steel flashed, hurtling end over end. At once, Red Hair's voice and words abruptly hung in the air, gurgled, and faded to silence. A stag-handled knife was now buried in his throat. An awful astonishment pervaded the scalp-hunter's features; his eyes were wide in amazement as he crumbled dead to the earth.

It was like an apparition, a confusing jungle of dimensionless sound and light, blurring colors, wavering figures, and then, gradually, crystal clarity. There she was:

my lovely sister, lying in the dust, bright tears rolling down her face, and her body shuddering uncontrollably.

I ran to her, unknotted the sharp rawhide laces that bit into her white wrists. Then, kneeling, holding Rebecca in my arms, I cried, "My shveste, my shveste." And Rebecca, in a state of shock, lifted her hands and gazed at them as if seeing them for the first time. For no longer was her skin—her tapering and elegant fingers, her joy and her pride—a perfection of smooth purity, but chafed flesh, bruised and scraped raw. Rebecca burst into heaving sobs, her face crumpled against my shoulder.

As I held Rebecca in my arms, rocking her back and forth like a child, Victorio, Lozen and the warriors walked among the dead and looted their bodies. They took guns, ammunition and tobacco, then rounded up the horses. They smiled and congratulated one another on a fine battle, a memorable victory, and there was valuable booty to share.

I said to Victorio, "I thought your warriors did not want to fight."

"Their hearts changed."

"Why?"

"I told them that Lozen is just a girl, but she puts them to shame. That she is a greater warrior. I told them that songs will be sung around our campfires about Lozen the woman warrior and they will be forgotten, like dust."

Shadows flew across the canyon floor. Shading my eyes, I looked up, squinted, and saw hungry vultures wheeling overhead.

Lozen approached and held out her hand, displaying more than a dozen double-eagle coins.

"You want?" she asked.

"What—who does that money belong to?"

"The dead."

I shook my head. I felt ill. To plunder the dead was wrong. Lozen shrugged; she rose and flung the coins away. The money painted a flaxen arc in the air, flashed in the sunlight, tiny golden mirrors, and then disappeared. The Apache believe that gold belongs in the sacred ground from where it came.

Lozen kneeled and tried to examine Rebecca's wounds. Frightened, Rebecca flinched and drew away from the Apache girl.

"It's all right," I told Rebecca soothingly. "Lozen is a medicine woman."

Rising, Lozen looked around, and walked to a low thorn bush. Cutting branches from the bush, she said to me, "This is called nopal leaf. With it I can treat her wounds."

Lozen knelt by a low fire; she burned the thorns from the leaf, split it and bound the fleshy side to Rebecca's torn flesh. I whispered little things to Rebecca and smoothed back her hair. She clung to me, shivering.

"It will heal in seven days," promised Lozen.

"I don't believe you," murmured Rebecca forlornly. "My hands, they will never, never ever, be the same."

"They will heal," insisted Lozen placidly. "They will heal and they will be more beautiful than ever. Some day, when you have a husband, he will hold your hands, and he will never suspect what happened to your skin."

Rebecca shook her head in wordless disbelief.

"Rebecca," I said, "when an Apache says something, it is the truth. Above all, Apache respect truth. So if Lozen says your hands will be healed, then you can be sure they will be healed."

"How do you know so much about the Apache?"

"Lozen has taught me."

"When did she do all this teaching, when did you do all this learning?"

"The past few weeks—in secret."

"And I thought I knew you, little brother."

"I thought I knew myself."

I stared at Lozen and Victorio. They had saved my life and my sister's, and I knew that I had to thank them, but for some reason I could not find the words to express my gratitude.

◎　◎　◎

Rebecca refused to ride on a horse by herself. She insisted on riding double with me. Her arms encircled my waist, held me tight. Her hot face rested between my shoulder blades. As we rode, I felt her heart beating, fluttering against my spine. Mile after mile we rode in silence. Swollen-eyed, she finally slept, and in her sleep, she whimpered. I dozed on and off, and every once in a while I felt myself slipping from the saddle, but Lozen was always by my side to make sure that I did not fall off.

"Why don't we stop and camp?" I begged, utterly exhausted.

Lozen explained that all the gunplay back at Apache Canyon would, no doubt, have alerted other bands of scalphunters in the area. Victorio did not want to take any chances; we were too close to Old Mexico, and he wanted to get out of the region as quickly as possible.

"Victorio has many enemies," said Lozen, smiling with pride.

On and on we rode through the furnace of daylight and into the ferocious chill of night. The distant mountains became dark smears. Birds cried intense and lonely songs. Crickets buzzed their mindless chatter. It was a mad and beautiful landscape, and my soul felt scoured clean. The stars sparkled violently and showered their silver light into the arms of bare upreaching cactus.

Rebecca stirred.

"Ariel?"

"Yes?"

"Just who are these Indians?"

"Victorio. This is Victorio. Don't you remember him from the Apache camp?"

Rebecca could only gape.

"I didn't recognize him. He looks like a demon."

"Not to me." I had grown accustomed to the fearsome look of the Apache warriors, to their bodies that were slick with glistening bear grease, to the bright and blazing war paint, to their long hair braided with smooth white animal bones.

"You saved my life."

"No, Victorio and Lozen saved your life."

"I am so ashamed."

"Of what?"

"Of how I used to make fun of you. I will never do it again." She nuzzled my cheek. I smiled, my heart swelling.

"Are Mama and Papa all right?"

"They are worried sick about you."

"This cannot go on, Ariel."

"What, what can't go on?"

"Papa. This endless journey. It has to stop."

"I know," I sighed. "Don't worry, Rebecca, our journey is almost over."

"Really?" she cried.

"Really," I assured her.

Lifting my head, I pushed on into the inky darkness as if motion itself were a purifying agent.

❧

Chapter 21

—· Forgotten ·—

A thin willow of smoke rose straight and undisturbed from Jeremiah and Keturah's adobe hut.

I raised the pistol in the air and fired off a warning shot to let them know that we were coming in. I did not want Jeremiah, frightened and clumsy as he was, to start shooting when he glimpsed Victorio and Lozen.

Mama and Papa peeked out from behind the wagon. They shielded their eyes from the brilliant needles of sunlight, cried out and ran to greet us.

Rebecca slid into Mama's arms. They held each other, their shadows joined and became one, a living portrait of rending tenderness. My bones ached. I felt glued to the saddle and simply sat there, gazing, as Papa stood next to me. He reached up and rested his hand on my knee.

"My son, my son," he said, shaking his head back and forth as if unable to quite believe his eyes.

"Papa."

"You look different, Ariel..."

"I am different, Papa, I am."

Incredulous, he asked, "How did you do it, how did you rescue your sister?"

"Lozen and Victorio did it," I explained. "Without them, Rebecca and I would have died."

"Those evil men, what has happened to them?"

"Dead, Papa, all dead."

Papa approached Victorio and Lozen.

"Thank you," Papa said, "I do not know how to thank you."

Victorio nodded and said, "There is a way. There is a way you can thank me."

"How?"

"God listens to you," said Victorio, "so you must speak to your God for Victorio."

"I pray to God, and I hope that he listens. There is no way of knowing if God answers my prayers."

Victorio said, "Will you speak to your God, for Victorio and for the Apache?"

"What do you want me to say?" Papa asked.

Victorio climbed down from his pony, took Papa by the arm and led him away. How fragile Papa looked beside the mighty war chief. Victorio leaned over and spoke urgently into Papa's ear. Papa listened, he stroked his beard, twisted his peyes, nodded his head, touched Victorio's powerful shoulder. Victorio and Papa walked down to the creek, deep in conversation. Later, Papa told me that Victorio wanted Papa to pray that when the time came, Victorio would die with honor and dignity. Victorio wanted Papa to pray that all the Apache warriors would die honorably at the hands of the white-eyes.

"Is death the only way?" Papa asked.

"The future is decided," said Victorio. "Death will come, but disgrace must be avoided."

Lozen slid from her horse and helped me dismount. I winced and groaned in pain; my muscles were locked in place. Mama loosened her grip on Rebecca, grabbed me by the arms and crushed me to her breast. Her flesh was warm as challah.

"So," she said, "look at my son, the Hebrew Kid. You probably think you are a real shtarker now, don't you?"

I shrugged. And suddenly I was twitching and crying. It was all a dizzy confusion.

"Pitzkeleh." Mama held and soothed me. Then she reached over, reeled in Lozen like a fish on a hook and hugged her tight. Lozen resisted for a moment, but Mama's arms were clamped stubbornly around her, and finally Lozen relented and let Mama's sturdy arms hold her.

"You may be a wild girl but we owe you everything. Name it, what can I give you?"

"Kugel," said Lozen. "I like your kugel."

◙　◙　◙

After eating, Victorio and Lozen said they would be heading out. It was time for them to get back to their camp.

"You cannot," protested Papa.

We all looked at him.

"Have you forgotten, Ariel, that today is your bar mitzvah?"

I had forgotten. I had lost track of time. Turning to Lozen, I begged her, "Stay, please stay for my bar mitzvah?"

Lozen looked to Victorio for a decision; he pondered a moment and then nodded his head in assent.

I would not have a minyan, but I would have the great Victorio and his sister Lozen as my guests.

◎ ◎ ◎

Nervously glancing at Victorio, Jeremiah and Keturah crept out of their cabin and set up some benches and chairs. Papa insisted on a mechitzah—a curtain separating the men from the women—although none of our guests were Jewish. So Keturah and Mama hung a sheet on a clothesline. It was almost like a real shul.

Papa and I started to pray. Victorio sat upright with the little siddur I had given to him in his large, beefy hands.

Just as we were about to say the Sh'ma, Victorio shot to his feet and, alarmed, looked north. A triangle of dust rose in the near distance. Riders were approaching.

"Who could be coming?" I asked Jeremiah.

"Closest neighbor's about twelve miles away, the Van der Brook family. But that's a considerable amount of dust. Could be cavalry from Fort Grant."

Immediately, Victorio chambered a round into his Henry rifle. Lozen ran to get their horses.

"Please," Papa pleaded, "no fighting."

But Victorio was already climbing to the roof of the shack and watching the incoming riders.

"He is an Apache war chief," I told Papa.

"Nu, and what does that mean?"

"It means that he is born to fight."

"Not on your bar mitzvah," Papa said through clenched teeth. "I will not have it," he vowed.

Lozen was checking the loads on the pistols she wore around her waist. Her face was grim, determined.

"Lozen, please."

"The blue coats want Victorio dead. We have to fight."

"Not today, Lozen, it doesn't have to be this way."

"It is how it is, Ariel."

"I don't want no part of this," exclaimed Jeremiah. He grabbed Keturah's hand, dashed inside the cabin and bolted the door.

I scrambled to the top of the bluff, watched the curtain of dust getting closer and closer. I was looking for the fluttering American flag, the cavalry pennants flapping in the wind.

If it was the army, there would be terrible bloodshed.

And, I asked myself, when the fighting started, where would I stand?

Chapter 22

—· Farewell ·—

Gradually, about fifteen riders rode into view through eddies of dust. They were all civilians. And I recognized the lead horseman.

"Do not shoot, Victorio," I cried. "Please do not shoot."

The riders came into the homestead. They were townspeople, solid citizens and shopkeepers in their three-piece suits and fine derby hats.

I called to the lead rider, "Hello, Doc."

Doc Holliday smiled, dismounted, and, always the Southern gentleman, bowed lavishly to Mama and Rebecca.

"I sincerely hope that we are not too late."

"Late for what?" I asked.

"Your bar mitzvah. It is today, is it not?"

I nodded.

"And you still need your quorum?"

Again, I nodded.

Doc swept his Stetson in the direction of the shopkeepers.

"Allow me to proudly present the Tombstone minyan."

A young man with a long mustache, the ends waxed to needle points, climbed down from his horse and came over to me. He spoke with a German accent.

"My name is Schwartz, Myron Schwartz. I run the haberdashery store in Tombstone. Are you the bar mitzvah boy?"

"Yes, I am."

Mr. Schwartz heaved a great sigh; it was most definitely a sigh of relief. "Okay, Doc, we owe you an apology."

Doc smiled and dipped his head in Schwartz's direction. "Mr. Schwartz and his Hebrew brethren thought that I was just a mad drunkard. Or worse."

"We did not know what to think. The story he told, well, it does not sound quite kosher, does it?"

"No, I suppose not," I said, shaking my head in amazement.

The other Tombstone Jews dismounted, and one by one they introduced themselves to me and to Papa. For the most part, they were prosperous Austrian and Prussian Jews, merchants and real estate dealers.

As the Tombstone minyan arranged themselves for prayer, I felt butterflies in my stomach. Doc took notice and came over to me.

"Thank you, Doc. Thank you so much." He smelled of rosewater and whiskey.

"Do you think Cousin Mattie would be proud of me?" he asked.

There it was, Doc's hunger for the smallest redemption.

"She would be very proud of you, Doc."

"I did a mitzvah, I surely did."

I nodded. Then Doc's body went rigid. The fingers of his right hand drummed against his thigh. It happened in the blink of an eye; his pistols were out and aimed right at Victorio. And Victorio's rifle was trained on Doc.

"No!" I cried.

The Tombstone Jews, all unarmed, dived for cover.

"That's Victorio!" Doc cried.

"He's my friend, Doc. He saved me. He saved Rebecca. Please put down your gun."

"Half the territory's contendin' for that savage," he snapped heatedly.

I blurted out the story. How the scalphunters came back and stole Rebecca. How Lozen saved me from thirst. How Victorio and his braves wiped out the evil vaqueros and scalphunters and rescued Rebecca.

"You are all guests at my bar mitzvah," I begged. "Please, put down your guns. Declare a peace treaty, just for now."

Doc and Victorio locked dark gazes. The moment of silence seemed to stretch into eternity.

◎ ◎ ◎

It was a strange sight, Doc Holliday and Victorio sitting side by side at my Bar Mitzvah ceremony. Utterly suspicious of one another, neither would agree to sit behind the other, so they were forced to sit together.

Lozen, Mama, Keturah and Rebecca shared a bench. Baby Gabriel slept in Mama's arms.

The Jews of Tombstone were not traditionally observant, but as the service continued, they started to join in the prayers with more and more enthusiasm. Memories of the old country, of their more religious parents and grand-parents, awakened feelings that had long been dormant or forgotten. Soon enough, they were saying the prayers with gusto, swaying back and forth, singing with real fervor.

The time came for me to chant the haftorah. My voice was surprisingly strong. Papa stood by my side; the fingers of his right hand rose and fell with the tune I sang. Out of the corner of my eye, I glanced at Lozen. She smiled at me.

After I said the haftorah, Papa addressed our peculiar congregation.

"My son, Ariel, is now bar mitzvah. From the bottom of my heart, I wish to thank all of you for being here, for making this minyan possible. Now it is traditional for the Bar Mitzvah boy to say a d'var Torah—some words of wisdom. Ariel?"

I stood there and stared at my bar mitzvah minyan. I had prepared a d'var Torah with Papa, a complicated Talmudic discourse, but abruptly I realized that it was no longer appropriate.

"Beloved family and friends," I began, "I want to tell you about the Lamed Vovniks, the thirty-six righteous men who are the pillars of the world. The rabbis tell us that without these righteous men, the world would not exist..."

Papa gave me a questioning look, but I continued: "Papa

and I have been searching for the Lamed Vovniks since we came to America. You see, back in Russia we suffered so much, saw so many Jews tortured and murdered that, well, I think that we became confused. Why was God doing this to us? What was His purpose?

"And so because we were confused, because we were frightened, and maybe because we had lost some of our faith, we decided to search for the thirty-six righteous men who wander the world performing good deeds. It was a hard and lonely journey. And I have to admit, after a while I no longer believed that they existed. I told myself that the story of the Lamed Vovniks is just a legend, a lovely aggadah, not to be taken literally. But this is not something that I could or would ever tell Papa."

Papa was staring at me, his eyes moist, filled with pain and longing.

"Yes, Papa, I stopped believing in your dream. I was ready to tell you to give up this search, that it was time for us to settle down in a town, live a normal life…"

"Stop," cried Mama, rising to her feet. "You are hurting your father, can't you see!"

"It's okay, Mama, just listen."

There was a low murmur from our guests.

I continued. "But Papa, I was wrong, and in a way, you were right. Righteous men and women do exist. They are not the Lamed Vovniks we normally think of, but for me they are close enough."

Papa sat forward, carefully listening.

"Look around, Papa. People very much like the Lamed Vovniks are among us. Lozen is one of them. She saved my life, Papa. Gave me water when I was dying. Victorio is one of them. He risked his life and the lives of his braves to rescue Rebecca from those evil men. Doc Holliday is one of them. Look how he gathered this holy minyan for no other reason than it was the right thing to do. And this wonderful Tombstone minyan; by coming out here and making a minyan, you all resemble the Lamed Vovniks. Keturah, Jeremiah, you too, yes, you too are righteous for sharing your home with us, complete strangers, so generously. The world may be filled with evil, but there is also goodness. All around us are men and women who do deeds of kindness when you least expect it. America is filled with such righteous people."

I do not know when it happened, but it seemed that everybody was crying. Even Victorio's dark onyx eyes were shining with tears.

My voice faded to silence. I looked at them all, and my heart whispered thank you.

From the sky came a beautiful angled beam of light, shimmering gold. A light desert breeze pushed against my face. It seemed as if it had taken me ages—lifetimes—to arrive at this moment.

I had come to America a child, and now, finally, I was a man.

◙ ◙ ◙

After the service, Mama served her cholent. "Mazel tov! Mazel tov!" cried the Tombstone Jews. My back was slapped; my cheeks were pinched. Doc Holliday raised his silver flask in toast.

Papa hugged me and told me that my bar mitzvah speech was inspired. "I suppose," he said, "that you no longer wish to search for the Lamed Vovniks."

"Papa," I said, "it's time to stop drifting. It's time to settle down in a real town and build a life like real Americans."

"Yes, yes, I suppose," said Papa.

"How else will Rebecca ever find a decent Jewish husband? And Gabriel, shouldn't he grow up in a town and not in a wagon? And what about Mama? Shouldn't she have a real home with curtains on the windows and a garden to grow flowers?"

"Tombstone?" said Papa.

"Mr. Schwartz says there's only one shoemaker for the whole town, and Tombstone is growing all the time. We could make a decent living there. We could help build a nice Jewish community."

"And what about you, Ariel, will you be happy in a town? Won't you miss your friend Lozen?"

That was the thing about Papa; he always knew, even before I did, the commotion in my heart.

Lozen. She was melded to my life. Her face, her words, her soul had become as much a part of me as my very own breath. Papa was right, and I was riven by the thought of moving to Tombstone and being separated from her.

I looked around for Lozen—but she was gone.

Lozen and Victorio had slipped away unseen.

My heart stirred, and I sprinted up the rise and to the trail until I caught sight of them as they rode away on their swift ponies.

"Lozen!" I cried. "Lozen!"

She halted, turned her horse around, and raised her arm in a gesture of—a gesture of what?

Was she finally saying goodbye?

Would I ever see her again?

Magically, across the yawning distance, I could see deep into her eyes. And her eyes were bidding me goodbye. Her eyes were telling me that our journey together was at an end. Her voice, which I heard as a whisper in my heart, was telling me that the time had come for the Hebrew Kid and the Apache Maiden to part.

Her horse rose on its hind legs, danced briskly from side to side. Dust boiled up and settled—and then she was gone.

Lozen disappeared, leaving only a fine and haunting afterimage.

My heart felt ruptured. I was alone in the great American wilderness, aching in the memory of her open heart, burning with the memory of our friendship.

❀

—·The End·—

—·· What Really Happened ··—

The settling of the American West and the Apache Wars have always been as much romantic legend as reliable history. The events of this story are fiction, but Victorio, Lozen and John Henry "Doc" Holliday did exist.

Doc Holliday was a complex and puzzling figure. It is true, however, that he was greatly attached to his pious cousin Mattie, who eventually did become a Catholic nun. Holliday claimed to have a degree in dentistry, although none of the three schools then in existence had records of his attendance. He was a deadly gunfighter and may have killed close to a dozen men in his career. Holliday was a gambler, a drunkard, and probably took part in several stagecoach robberies. Eventually, he did marry Big Nose Kate Elder. Holliday was a close and loyal friend to Wyatt Earp, and the gunfight at the OK Corral has been portrayed in book and film countless times. Holliday died of tuberculosis in 1887.

Lozen was Victorio's younger sister and was greatly respected as a fighter, medicine woman and midwife. She was invited to sit at war councils and was probably a major participant in every Warm Springs or Chiricahua conflict during the 1870s and 1880s. At her puberty rites, she earned her power during a vigil on a sacred mountain. Reliable testimony relates that she was able to enter a trance and "locate" her enemies. Lozen has been described as "very beautiful," and many young warriors asked Victorio's permission to marry her, but Lozen begged her brother not to order her to marry, and she never took a husband—most unusual for an Apache maiden.

Victorio was a great and remarkably successful Apache war chief. His masterful battlefield strategy and tactics are a model for guerilla warfare. Several American army officers considered Victorio the greatest Indian general who had ever appeared on the American continent. Victorio earned the respect of the whites who fought him and retained the love and respect of those who followed him. In 1880 Victorio and his band were trapped and massacred in the Tres Castillo Mountains in Chihuahua, Mexico. Victorio committed suicide rather than suffer capture or death at the hands of the white man. He died with honor, just as he wished.

In 1886, Geronimo, the last Apache on the warpath, surrendered to the United States Army. With Geronimo's tiny band of exhausted and half-starved Apache warriors was one brave and obstinate woman, Lozen. She was defiant in the face of the overwhelming odds and implored Geronimo not to surrender.

Lozen and the other Apache prisoners were moved to

the swampy, mosquito-infested Mount Vernon Barracks in Alabama. There, Lozen died of the "coughing sickness," probably tuberculosis. She was buried in an unmarked grave.

Thousands of Jews seeking freedom and better lives took part in the westward expansion of America. They were as varied in their occupations as all other immigrant groups. There were Jewish traders, soldiers, shopkeepers, lawmen and lawbreakers. Some Jews married Native Americans and became vocal advocates for the rights of the displaced tribes.

Ariel and his family are fiction, but their attitudes, fears, and conflicts are quite real.

They were all extraordinarily brave people—the Apache and the white settlers—and it is a great tragedy that this land was not large enough for both people to exist peacefully side by side.

For further reading:

Pioneer Jews by Harriet and Fred Rochlin

In the Days of Victorio: Recollections of a Warm Springs Apache, and *Indeh: An Apache Odyssey*, both by Eve Ball

Illustrated Life of Doc Holliday, by G.G. Boyer

"Doc Holliday's Georgia Background," by Albert S. Pendleton Jr. and Susan McKey, *Journal of Arizona History*, *Vol. XIV, No. 3* (Autumn 1973)

—·Glossary·—

aggadah – Legend.

Alenu – The concluding prayer to the three daily services.

beis midrash – House of study.

bar mitzvah – The status of religious responsibility reached by a Jewish boy when he becomes thirteen years of age.

blood libel – A false accusation of ritual murder: that Jews use Christian blood as part of the Passover service.

bracha – Hebrew: a blessing.

bris milah, bris – The circumcision ceremony. Literally: the covenant of circumcision.

challah – The white bread loaf eaten on the Sabbath and Jewish festivals.

chossen – Yiddish: bridegroom.

cholent – Yiddish: a slow-cooked stew made from meat, potatoes and beans, traditionally served on Shabbos afternoon.

Devorah – Jewish prophetess and judge (Judges, Chapters 4-5).

d'var Torah– Comments on Torah. Literally: a word of Torah.

Even Ha-ezer– Codification of Jewish law regarding marriage. Authored by Rabbi Joseph Caro of Safed, Israel, sixteenth century.

daven– Yiddish: to pray.

davening– Yiddish: praying.

Goliath– Philistine war giant who was defeated in battle by the young and future King David.

goyim– Non-Jews. Literally, other nations.

haftorah– The passage from the Prophets read in the synagogue after reading the Torah on Shabbos and festivals.

halacha– Jewish law.

hesped– Eulogy.

Kabbalah– Jewish mystical thought.

Kaddish– A prayer that is said by the bereaved.

kallah– Bride.

kashrus– The Jewish dietary laws.

kesubah– The Jewish marriage contract.

King David– Second King of Israel.

kosher– According to the Jewish dietary laws.

kugel– Yiddish: pie. A delicacy made from potatoes, noodles or various other ingredients.

Lamed Vovniks – The "thirty-six"; in Jewish mystical thought, the world continues to exist because of the good deeds that are performed by thirty-six righteous men.

Glossary

landsman – Yiddish: fellow Jew.

Ma'ariv – The evening service.

maidel – Yiddish: little girl.

Maimonides – Moshe ben Maimon, rabbi, doctor and philosopher. Spain-Egypt (1135-1204).

mameleh – Yiddish: term of endearment for a beloved child.

mazel tov – Hebrew: congratulations.

meshugah – Hebrew: crazy.

mechitzah – A partition that separates men and women in a synagogue.

mezuzah – Small parchment with biblical passages attached to the doorpost.

minyan – The quorum of ten males over the age of thirteen required for public Jewish worship.

Mishnah – A work completed about 200 C.E. that codifies Jewish oral tradition since the Torah. It is the basic part of the Talmud.

mitzvah – Commandment from the Torah or the Sages. In popular speech, it has come to mean a good deed.

mohel – One qualified to perform ritual circumcision.

oysgegrient – Yiddish: un-green, more assimilated, more of an American.

Oy vey – Yiddish: woe is me.

peyes – Sidelocks worn by some observant Jewish men. The custom originates from Leviticus 19:27.

pitzkeleh – Yiddish: term of endearment, cutie-pie.

pogrom–Russian: an organized massacre of Jews. Pogroms were often sparked by blood libels.

power–Apache term for a prophetic or divine spirit.

semicha–Rabbinic ordination.

seraphim–The first order of the angels in Jewish tradition.

sha-shtill–Yiddish: be quiet and still.

Shabbos–The Sabbath. From sundown Friday until sundown Saturday.

Shacharis–The morning service.

shicksah–Yiddish: a gentile woman.

sheydim–Hebrew: demons, spirits.

sheygitz–Yiddish: a gentile man.

shidduch–Yiddish: an arranged marriage.

Sh'ma–The paragraph in the Bible that starts with "Hear, O Israel" (Deuteronomy 6:4-9). A declaration for the Jewish people that God is One.

shtarker–Yiddish: tough guy, big shot.

shtetl–Small Jewish village in Europe.

shul–Yiddish: synagogue.

Shulchan Aruch–Comprehensive code of Jewish law, compiled by Rabbi Joseph Caro of Safed, Israel, in the sixteenth century.

Shmoneh Esrei–The eighteen benedictions, the central portion of the daily prayers.

shmutzik–Yiddish: dirty, filthy.

shveste – Yiddish: sister.

siddur – Hebrew: a prayer book.

sitra achra – Kabbalistic notion of "the other side." A state of negative energy.

ta'anis – Literally, "fast." The volume of the Talmud that discusses the laws of fasting.

tante – Yiddish: aunt.

tallis – A prayer shawl.

Talmud – A voluminous compilation of the Oral Law based on the Mishnah.

Tehillim – The Book of Psalms, authored by King David.

Tefillin – Phylacteries. Two small leather boxes, one attached to the forehead and the other to the left arm, worn by observant Jewish men during the morning service every day except for the Sabbath and holidays. Each box contains strips of parchment inscribed with the following Hebrew passages from the Torah: Exodus 13: 1-10, Exodus 13: 11-16, Deuteronomy 6: 4-9, Deuteronomy 11: 13-21.

Torah – The five books of Moses: Genesis, Exodus, Leviticus, Numbers, and Deuteronomy. More broadly, all Jewish learning and tradition.

tochter – Yiddish: daughter.

treif – Yiddish: not kosher.

tushy – Rear end.

tzitzis – Fringes on the corners of the tallis (Numbers 15:38).

Ussen – Literally: Creator of Life. The Apache name for God.

Yael – A Jewish woman who, probably inspired by the prophetess Devorah, killed King Sisera, an enemy of the Jewish people (Judges 4:21).

Yom Kippur – The holiest day of the year, on which Jews atone for their sins.

Zohar – The most widely known book of Jewish mysticism, authored by Rabbi Shimon bar Yochai, an early sage of the Talmud.

About the Author

Robert J. Avrech is a screenwriter and producer in
Hollywood. Among his best known films are,
Body Double, directed by Brian DePalma and
A Stranger Among Us, directed by Sidney Lumet.
For his adaptation of the young adult classic, *The
Devil's Arithmetic*, Mr. Avrech won the Emmy
Award. He lives with his wife and children in Los
Angeles. This is Mr. Avrech's first novel.